BECOMING THE DIVINE YOU

Awaken the Power Within to Find True Happiness.

BALVINDER NATH

BlueRose ONE .com
Stories Matter
NewDelhi • London

BLUEROSE PUBLISHERS
India | U.K.

BlueRose ONE.com
Stories Matter
NewDelhi • London

For permissions requests or inquiries regarding this publication, please contact:

BLUEROSE PUBLISHERS
www.BlueRoseONE.com
info@bluerosepublishers.com
+91 8882 898 898
+4407342408967

ISBN: 978-93-7018-939-3

Cover design: Yash Singhal

First Edition: June 2025

The journey within is the most sacred pilgrimage for in knowing the self, we come to know the divine

Balvindernath Chaganla

Foreword

In the darkest phases of my life, I searched for someone to guide me out of the shadows. But I realized that the only way forward was through self-expression. Writing became my refuge, a way to bring clarity to my thoughts and illuminate my inner world.

This journey of spirituality began with words and deepened through travel. Exploring diverse cultures, faiths, and beliefs expanded my understanding of existence. Through it all, writing remained my constant companion, helping me process and express my spiritual growth.

These reflections trace back to my childhood in boarding school, away from family and shaped by circumstances beyond my control. Over the past ten years, yoga and meditation have become integral to my daily life, further refining my thoughts and deepening my connection to the divine self.

None of this would have been possible without my father's wisdom and guidance. His teachings have been my foundation, and I dedicate this book to him.

May this Book offer light to those navigating their own darkness, as they once did for me.

Prologue: The Art of Being

In the grand narrative of existence, there lies a paradox that has fascinated thinkers, poets, and seekers across millennia: the pursuit of fulfillment in a world marked by impermanence. What does it mean to truly live? Is it in the ceaseless chase of ambition, the quiet moments of introspection, or the connections we forge with others? Perhaps the answer lies not in choosing one path but in harmonizing all facets of our being.

This book is an exploration of that harmony. It is not a guide to living but an invitation to engage with life itself—an appeal to embrace its complexity, its beauty, and its inherent contradictions. To live fully is to navigate the delicate balance between thought and action, feeling and reason, self and other.

The Framework of Being

Human existence is a tapestry woven from the threads of thoughts, feelings, actions, and aspirations. At its core is the interplay of two profound forces: awareness and intention. Awareness allows us to see life as it is, free from the distortions of fear, ego, and assumption. Intention gives us the power to shape our reality, to craft meaning in a universe indifferent to our desires.

This duality—seeing and shaping—is the foundation of a purposeful life. To observe without judgment is to understand. To act with intention is to transform. Together, they create a dynamic equilibrium, a rhythm that propels us toward self-actualization while keeping us grounded in the present.

The Dance of Thought and Feeling

We are not merely thinkers, nor are we purely emotional beings. We are the confluence of intellect and emotion, rationality and intuition. Our thoughts shape our perceptions, yet it is our feelings that give life its color and depth.

The challenge lies in navigating these realms without becoming enslaved by either. A mind untethered by emotion risks cold detachment; a heart unmoored by reason may lead us astray. Wisdom emerges from the synergy of the two—a recognition that thought and feeling are not adversaries but allies in our quest for understanding.

The Philosophy of Presence

At the heart of this exploration is the practice of presence. To be present is to engage fully with the now, to resist the pull of regret for what was and anxiety for what might be. Presence is not passivity; it is an active state of alignment with reality, a willingness to meet life on its terms.

In presence, we discover the art of being. We learn to savor the simple joys—a sunrise, a kind word, a moment of silence. We also learn to face life's inevitable sorrows with grace and resilience. Presence teaches us that every experience, whether joyous or painful, is a chapter in the story of our becoming.

The Role of Connection

At the heart of this exploration is the practice of presence. To be present is to engage fully with the now, to resist the pull of regret for what was and anxiety for what might be. Presence is not passivity; it is an active state of alignment with reality, a willingness to meet life on its terms.

In presence, we discover the art of being. We learn to savor the simple joys—a sunrise, a kind word, a moment of silence. We also learn to face life's inevitable sorrows with grace and resilience. Presence teaches us that every experience, whether joyous or painful, is a chapter in the story of our becoming.

The Journey Ahead

This book is a compass, not a map. It does not prescribe a singular path but offers perspectives, insights, and tools to navigate the terrain of your own life. It is a conversation between the pages and the reader—a dialogue that evolves as you bring your own experiences, questions, and reflections to its words.

As you journey through its chapters, you will encounter ideas drawn from philosophy, neuroscience, psychology, and spirituality. These disciplines, though distinct, converge in their pursuit of a common goal: to understand the human condition and illuminate the path to fulfillment.

The ultimate aim of this book is not to provide answers but to inspire inquiry. It seeks to awaken in you a sense of curiosity, a desire to explore the depths of your own being and the world around you. For it is in the act of questioning, of seeking, that we find the seeds of transformation.

A Call to Presence

Before you begin, pause. Take a moment to center yourself, to breathe deeply, and to acknowledge the present. The words you are about to read are not just ink on paper; they are an invitation to engage with life more fully, more intentionally.

Remember, this is not a journey of perfection but of progress. There will be detours and challenges, moments of clarity and confusion. Embrace them all, for they are the raw materials of growth.

The art of being is not about arriving at a destination but about embracing the journey itself. It is about finding beauty in the ordinary, meaning in the mundane, and purpose in the process.

Let this book be a companion on that journey—a guide not to who you should be, but to who you already are.

CHAPTER 1: GOD IS YOU

Introduction to God is You

The concept of God has been a central theme in human existence for centuries, transcending cultures, religions, and philosophies. For many, God represents an omnipotent being who governs the universe and serves as a source of comfort, guidance, and purpose. But what if we shifted our perspective? What if, instead of looking outward, we turned inward to discover the divine within ourselves? This chapter explores the profound idea that God is You—a concept rooted in self-awareness, faith, and the interconnectedness of all existence.

To understand this notion, we must first examine the relationship between faith, thought, and belief. Faith is often seen as an external reliance on a higher power, but in truth, it begins within. It is a reflection of our innermost thoughts and beliefs, which in turn shape our perception of reality. When we place faith in ourselves, we unlock the ability to manifest our desires, overcome challenges, and experience life with a sense of purpose. This is not to dismiss the existence of a higher power but to emphasize that divinity resides in each of us as a part of a larger cosmic cycle.

The idea of "God is You" invites us to see ourselves as active participants in the creation of our lives. It challenges us to embrace trust, love, abundance, and wisdom as intrinsic qualities rather than external gifts. It also prompts us to question traditional notions of divinity that often place God as a separate entity to be worshiped. Instead, it encourages us to recognize the divine spark within and cultivate a life rooted in self-respect, joy, and compassion.

A key aspect of this philosophy is understanding the role of thought. Thoughts are powerful tools that shape our actions, decisions, and ultimately, our destiny. When we align our thoughts with positive emotions and intentions, we create a ripple effect that enhances not only our own lives but also those around us. Conversely, negative thoughts rooted in fear can limit our potential and perpetuate cycles of pain and doubt. This chapter delves into how embracing the divine within can help us transform our thought patterns, shifting from fear-based reactions to love-driven responses.

Another essential element is the interplay between devotion and passion. Traditionally, devotion is associated with religious rituals and practices aimed at pleasing a deity. However, when viewed through the lens of "God is You," devotion takes on a new meaning. It becomes a commitment to oneself—a dedication to nurturing one's physical, mental, and spiritual well-being. This chapter explores how passion, when channeled effectively, becomes a form of devotion that drives us toward our highest potential.

Ultimately, "God is You" is not about negating the existence of a higher power but about redefining it. It is an invitation to embark on a journey of self-discovery, to see the divine in every aspect of life, and to live with intention and authenticity. By embracing this philosophy, we open ourselves to a deeper understanding of who we are and the limitless possibilities that lie within.

GOD IS FAITH
FAITH IS BELIEF.
BELIEF IS THOUGHT.
THE THOUGHT COMES FROM YOU.
THUS, "THOUGHT = GOD"

God is a cycle where you are on both ends. The creator and the created. The believer and the believed. The seeker and the sought.

The Origin of God:

God, as we understand it, is an invention of the human mind. In the early days of humanity, when people gathered around fires and sought meaning in the stars, **God was born**, not as a figure of judgment, but **as a source of hope**, unity, and strength. God was invented to provide solace to groups of people—a symbol of shared faith to face the mysteries of existence.

Yet, as societies evolved, the idea of God diversified. Different cultures and communities envisioned God in ways that resonated with their experiences. Some saw God in the sun, others in the ocean, and some in the unseen forces of nature. But at its core, God remained a projection of the human desire to trust, love, and find purpose.

The essence of God was never static. It evolved with humanity. From being a representation of natural forces to becoming an abstract concept of love, wisdom, and justice, God mirrored the human journey. Understanding this evolution helps us see that God has always been a reflection of who we are.

Discovering God Within

If God is an invention, then the ultimate discovery is realizing that God resides within you. To find God, you must look inward. God is not an external entity to be worshipped but an internal force to be embraced. By being your truest self, you uncover the divine essence within you.

Focus on the virtues that connect you to this divinity:

- **Trust:** Believe in yourself and others. Trust creates a foundation for love and harmony.
- **Love:** The purest expression of God. To love and to be loved is to experience the divine.
- **Abundance:** Recognize that the universe provides enough for everyone. Scarcity is a construct of fear.
- **Peace:** Find calmness within. When your mind is at peace, you align with God.

- **Self-respect:** Honor yourself as a reflection of the divine.
- **Freedom:** God's essence is liberation—freedom from fear, doubt, and limitations.
- **Joy and Laughter:** God is present in moments of happiness. Laughter is a direct connection to your soul.

Negative emotions, on the other hand, stem from fear. Fear clouds your connection to God. When you let go of fear, you open yourself to trust, love, and abundance.

Thought = You, Thought = God

If thoughts originate from you, and thoughts shape your reality, then your thoughts are divine. When you think of God, you are channeling the power of your own mind. But thoughts are not passive. They are powerful forces that shape the world around you.

- **Positive thoughts** create growth, healing, and happiness.
- **Negative thoughts** attract doubt, despair, and stagnation.

When you serve God, you are, in essence, serving your higher self. Remedies to the mind come from acts of devotion. But devotion is not limited to rituals or prayers; it is passion—a wholehearted dedication to something greater than yourself.

The Illusion of Faith

Faith is a fascinating concept. It often manifests as an illusionary figure, a mental construct that gives shape to our thoughts. God becomes the name we give to this faith. Across the world, people create different Gods to represent their faith—each tailored to their cultural and emotional needs.

Faith, however, is universal. It is the glue that binds humanity. It is the invisible thread connecting our thoughts, actions, and outcomes. Whether you call it God, energy, or simply belief, it is the same force that moves mountains and inspires revolutions.

Faith's true power lies in its ability to transform lives. It is not bound by religion or dogma. It is a personal journey that connects you to your higher self and the world around you.

The Healing Power of Thought

When you are hurt, you instinctively look outward for someone or something to heal you. This act of expectation delays the healing process. The body, like the mind, responds to signals. If you tell your body to wait, it will wait. If you tell it to heal, it will heal.

Desperation to heal is not weakness; it is a powerful signal to your body to activate its natural mechanisms. The same applies to emotional wounds. The more you focus on healing, the faster your mind will align with that goal.

Understanding this principle is transformative. It teaches you to take charge of your well-being and recognize the immense power within you to heal and grow.

The Power of Asking

At temples, people often ask God what they want. They pour out their desires, hopes, and dreams. But outside the temple, they do the opposite. They talk about what they don't want. They dwell on their fears, frustrations, and failures.

This creates a paradox. By focusing on what you don't want, you inadvertently attract it. The mind, much like the universe, responds to repetition. The more you repeat a thought, the more you reinforce it. Thus, talking about your fears brings them closer, while talking about your desires brings them to life.

The lesson here is simple: talk about what you want. Speak your dreams into existence. Align your thoughts, words, and actions with your aspirations, and watch the universe conspire to help you achieve them.

Your words hold immense power. They shape your reality. Use them wisely.

Devotion = Passion

Devotion is often misunderstood as blind faith or ritualistic worship. In reality, devotion is passion. It is the wholehearted commitment to a purpose, person, or idea. When you are devoted, you channel your energy into something meaningful. This creates a sense of fulfillment and aligns you with the divine.

Think of devotion as a flame. It can light up your path, inspire others, and even transform the world. Whether your devotion is directed toward art, science, relationships, or self-improvement, it connects you to God by unlocking your highest potential.

Devotion transforms mundane actions into sacred rituals. It elevates your purpose and infuses your life with meaning.

Practical Steps to Realize "God is You"

1. **Practice Self-Reflection:** Spend time in silence. Reflect on your thoughts, emotions, and actions. This helps you recognize the divine within.
2. **Focus on Positivity:** Train your mind to dwell on positive thoughts. Replace fear with trust, anger with love, and doubt with confidence.
3. **Serve Others:** Acts of kindness and generosity strengthen your connection to God. By serving others, you serve yourself.
4. **Speak Your Desires:** Be mindful of your words. Speak about what you want, not what you fear.
5. **Embrace Devotion:** Find something you are passionate about and dedicate yourself to it. Let your devotion guide your actions.
6. **Heal from Within:** Trust your body and mind to heal themselves. Send positive signals and believe in their power.
7. **Gratitude Practice:** Acknowledge the blessings in your life. Gratitude amplifies positivity and deepens your connection to God.
8. **Live Authentically:** Be true to yourself. Authenticity is the purest expression of divinity.

The Cycle of God

God is not a distant entity; God is a cycle. A loop where faith, thought, and action come full circle. You are both the creator and the created. The cycle begins and ends with you.

When you realize this, you unlock the ultimate truth:

- God is not in the sky; God is in your heart.
- God is not in rituals; God is in your actions.
- God is not in separation; God is in unity.

By embracing this philosophy, you transcend the illusion of God as an external force and discover the divine essence within yourself. You become the God you seek.

Expanding the Horizon: You as the Creator

The belief that "God is You" isn't confined to philosophical reflection; it's a call to action. If you are the creator, what will you create? What kind of world do you want to build? This realization empowers you to take responsibility for your thoughts and actions, shaping a life that aligns with your highest aspirations.

- **Creating Abundance:** Start by believing that there is enough for everyone. Share what you have and watch how abundance multiplies.
- **Healing Relationships:** Forgive and seek forgiveness. Healing broken relationships is a divine act.
- **Building Community:** Unite people around shared goals and values. Communities thrive on trust, love, and shared purpose.
- **Innovating Solutions:** Use your talents to solve problems. Creativity is a divine expression.

By stepping into the role of the creator, you not only change your life but also influence the world around you. Every action, no matter how small, contributes to the larger cycle of creation.

"The divine resides not in the heavens or the rituals we follow, but in the thoughts we think, the actions we take, and the love we share. To see God, look within; to serve God, live with purpose. You are the creator of your own destiny, the author of your own story, and the God of your own universe."

CHAPTER 2: LANGUAGE IS EXPRESSION

Introduction: Language is Expression

Language is the most profound tool of human connection, a bridge between the inner world of thoughts and the external reality we share. It transcends mere words, embodying imagination, emotion, and the limitless potential of human creativity. Through language, we craft meaning, communicate ideas, and breathe life into the unseen. It is both a reflection of who we are and a canvas for who we aspire to be.

"Language is the art of turning thoughts into reality, a bridge that connects the unseen within us to the world around us."

Language is the Bridge

Language is a remarkable phenomenon, transcending its role as a mere collection of words. It is the essence of human communication, the tool through which we connect, and the framework upon which we build relationships, societies, and civilizations. But beyond its functional aspects, language is a bridge—one that connects the visible to the invisible, the tangible to the intangible, and the known to the unknown. It is a manifestation of our imagination and the vehicle that carries our thoughts into the realm of possibility.

Language as a Manifestation of Imagination

At its core, language is born from imagination. Every word, phrase, and sentence we speak is a reflection of the thoughts that take shape in our minds. Before the invention of words, humans relied on gestures, symbols, and sounds to convey meaning. Yet, as our consciousness evolved, so did our need to express complex ideas, emotions, and dreams. This need gave rise to language, enabling us to articulate the ineffable and share our inner worlds with others.

Through language, we give form to the intangible. Concepts like love, hope, justice, and freedom are abstract and ungraspable without the words that define them. Language allows us to capture these ideas and bring them into the realm of understanding. It bridges the gap between thought and expression, allowing us to dream, create, and innovate. Without language, imagination would remain confined within the boundaries of our minds, unable to influence the world around us.

The Power of Words to Shape Reality

Language does not merely describe reality; it shapes it. Words carry immense power, capable of influencing emotions, thoughts, and actions. They can inspire revolutions, heal wounds, and unite nations. Conversely, they can also divide, harm, and destroy. This duality highlights the responsibility that comes with using language.

Consider the words of great leaders and thinkers throughout history. Their speeches, writings, and ideas have shaped societies and transformed cultures. Mahatma Gandhi's call for nonviolence, Martin Luther King Jr.'s dream of equality, and Rabindranath Tagore's poetic vision of freedom—all were brought to life through language. These examples illustrate how words can transcend time and space, becoming bridges that connect generations and ideologies.

Language as a Tool for Connection

Language is fundamentally relational. It enables us to connect with others, to share our stories, and to understand the experiences of those who are different from us. It is through language that we form communities, build trust, and create bonds that transcend individual differences.

In this sense, language is not just a bridge between thoughts but also between people. When we speak, write, or even gesture, we are reaching out to others, inviting them to step into our world. This connection is not limited to spoken or written language; it extends to the many ways humans express themselves—through art, music, dance, and design. Each of these forms of expression is a language in its own right, offering a unique bridge to understanding.

Moreover, language allows us to empathize. By listening to others and engaging with their words, we gain insights into their experiences, struggles, and aspirations. This empathy is the foundation of compassion and cooperation, enabling us to build a more inclusive and harmonious world.

The Role of Language in Creativity and Innovation

Language is the engine of creativity. It provides the structure and vocabulary necessary to articulate new ideas and concepts. Without language, innovation would be stifled, as there would be no way to communicate or refine novel thoughts.

Consider the world of science and technology. Theories, discoveries, and inventions rely on language to be documented, shared, and built upon. The very act of naming a phenomenon—whether it is gravity, relativity, or artificial intelligence—gives it a place in our collective understanding. Language thus becomes the bridge that connects individual genius to collective progress.

In the arts, language is equally vital. Poets, novelists, and playwrights use words to paint vivid landscapes of emotion and imagination. Even in visual and performing arts, where the medium may not involve traditional language, the concepts and narratives often begin with words. Language serves as the foundation upon which creativity is constructed, enabling artists to explore the depths of human experience and share their vision with the world.

Language as a Bridge to the Future

Language is not only a reflection of the present but also a tool for shaping the future. When we use language, we are not merely describing what is; we are also envisioning what could be. This forward-looking aspect of language is evident in goal-setting, planning, and storytelling.

Through language, we communicate our aspirations and chart the path toward achieving them. For instance, a mission statement or a manifesto articulates a vision for the future, inspiring others to work toward its realization. Similarly, storytelling allows us to imagine alternate realities, exploring possibilities that challenge the status quo and open new avenues for growth.

Language also connects us to our future selves. The words we use today—whether in journals, letters, or even internal dialogue—serve as a bridge to the person we are becoming. By expressing our dreams and intentions, we lay the groundwork for their fulfillment.

The Ethical Use of Language

Given its immense power, the use of language comes with ethical responsibilities. Language should be a force for good, promoting appreciation, generosity, and gratitude. When we use words to uplift, encourage, and inspire, we create bridges of understanding and cooperation.

Conversely, language can also be weaponized. Words of hatred, deceit, or manipulation can erode trust and sow discord. Recognizing this potential, we must strive to use language with integrity, ensuring that it reflects our highest values and intentions.

The ethical use of language also extends to its inclusivity. Language should be a bridge that welcomes all, rather than a barrier that excludes. By embracing diversity in language—whether through the inclusion of marginalized voices or the use of gender-neutral terms—we can create a more equitable and compassionate world.

Language as a Reflection of the Divinet

For many, language is a spiritual experience, a reflection of the divine within us. The ability to express thoughts, emotions, and ideas is seen as a gift, a reminder of our connection to a higher power. In this context, language becomes a form of worship, a way of honoring the creativity and wisdom imbued in humanity.

Through prayer, meditation, and sacred texts, language serves as a bridge to the divine. It allows us to articulate our faith, seek guidance, and find solace in moments of uncertainty. This spiritual dimension of language underscores its role as a bridge not only between humans but also between the mortal and the eternal.

Faith and Fear

Faith and fear are two profound forces that shape the human experience. At first glance, they may seem like opposites—faith as a source of courage and fear as a cause of hesitation. Yet, these forces are intricately intertwined, each playing a vital role in our journey toward self-discovery and belief. The journey to believe in the faith of God—who is, in essence, you—requires embracing both fear and acceptance. Together, they become the catalysts for transformation, enabling us to move from doubt to conviction and from conviction to action.

Fear as a Guide

Fear often carries a negative connotation, associated with weakness, avoidance, or failure. However, fear is not inherently an obstacle; it is a signal, a guide that illuminates the areas in our lives where growth is needed. When we encounter fear, it is a reflection of our vulnerabilities, uncertainties, and the limits we have unconsciously set for ourselves.

To acknowledge fear is to face it with honesty. This acknowledgment does not mean succumbing to fear but rather using it as a mirror to understand our deepest anxieties and aspirations. For instance, the fear of failure often reveals a deep desire for success, while the fear of rejection highlights the longing for connection and acceptance. Fear, when approached with curiosity and courage, becomes a teacher, showing us the path to overcome our limitations and step into our potential.

Acceptance as a Pathway

While fear points to where we must grow, acceptance provides the strength to take the first step forward. Acceptance is not about resignation or passivity;

it is an active acknowledgment of the present moment, including its challenges, imperfections, and uncertainties. It is through acceptance that we make peace with our fears and begin to transform them into opportunities for growth.

Acceptance allows us to let go of resistance and judgment, clearing the way for clarity and focus. When we accept our fears, we no longer waste energy fighting or avoiding them. Instead, we channel that energy into constructive action. This process transforms thoughts into belief, as acceptance builds the foundation of trust—trust in ourselves, in the journey, and in the higher power that resides within us.

Faith as the Union of Fear and Acceptance

Faith is born at the intersection of fear and acceptance. It is the act of believing not despite fear, but because of it. Faith acknowledges the presence of fear and embraces the courage to move forward anyway. It is an inner knowing that every challenge we face is an opportunity to grow stronger, wiser, and closer to our true selves.

Believing in the faith of God—who is you—is an act of profound self-trust. It is the realization that the divine is not external but within, guiding you through every moment of uncertainty. When fear is embraced as a guide and acceptance as a pathway, faith becomes a force that empowers you to transform your thoughts into actions and your dreams into reality.

Expression is Energy

Expression is the outward flow of energy, a dynamic force that bridges the internal world of thoughts, emotions, and vitality with the external world of action, creation, and communication. Every aspect of life—movement, speech, art, and even the unseen workings of our bodies—is a manifestation of this energy in motion. Expression is not merely a tool for interaction but a profound way to transform intangible energies into tangible forms, making the invisible visible.

Life as Expression

The functioning of our organs, for instance, is an expression of life itself. The rhythmic beating of the heart, the steady flow of breath, and the intricate communication between cells are silent yet powerful affirmations of existence. Each function reflects the vitality within us, a harmonious interplay of energy that sustains life.

Similarly, the movement of a body part, whether it's a purposeful gesture or a subconscious action, speaks volumes about the energy coursing through us. A simple smile, a wave, or a stride forward is an outward sign of vitality and intent.

Art as Expression

Art, in all its forms, is perhaps the most universal and timeless expression of energy. From a painting that captures a fleeting emotion to a melody that stirs the soul, art transforms inner experiences into creations that resonate with others. It is through art that the energy of passion, pain, joy, or hope finds its voice, connecting people across cultures and generations.

Expression as Communication

Expression is the foundation of how we communicate and connect with the world. Words, gestures, and even silence are tools through which we convey meaning, emotion, and intent. These outward manifestations of energy are not random but deeply purposeful, allowing us to form relationships, share ideas, and leave lasting impressions.

Expression is also a transformative force. By expressing our thoughts and feelings, we gain clarity, release tension, and create space for growth. It allows us to channel our inner energy into constructive outlets, fostering creativity, empathy, and understanding.

The Essence of Expression

At its core, expression is energy in motion—a force that flows through every aspect of life. It is how we leave our mark on the world, turning the abstract into the concrete, the fleeting into the eternal. Whether through art, movement, or simple everyday actions, expression is the heartbeat of human existence, a testament to the vitality within us.

Passion is Rhythm

Passion is the rhythm of energy within you, a pulse that shapes your actions, decisions, and creations. It is born from moments of intense emotion, shaped by your experiences and aspirations. Passion is not a fleeting feeling but a steady force that drives you to express, connect, and achieve. It is the rhythm that gives your energy direction, purpose, and resonance.

Passion Through Movement

One of the most immediate ways passion manifests is through the movements of the body. Dance, for example, is a direct expression of rhythm, translating inner energy into graceful, powerful, or joyous motion. Even in everyday actions—whether it's a determined stride or an excited gesture—passion reveals itself as the rhythm that animates our physical form.

Amplifying Passion with Instruments

Instruments are also powerful channels for passion. A musical instrument amplifies the rhythm within, turning invisible feelings into audible vibrations. Similarly, tools of art—like brushes, pens, or chisels—extend the reach of passion, transforming raw energy into tangible creations. These instruments allow passion to transcend the boundaries of the individual, reaching others and inspiring them.

Passion in Art, Design, and Language

Art, design, and language are structured forms of passion. They give shape to emotions and ideas, creating something that can be shared and understood. A painting can evoke awe, a well-crafted design can inspire innovation, and words can move hearts and minds. Through these mediums, passion becomes a universal language, connecting people and igniting collective energy.

The Rhythm of Moments

Passion is not static; it ebbs and flows with the moments that define our lives. A triumphant success, a profound loss, or even a quiet realization can set the rhythm of passion in motion. Each moment adds a new beat to the rhythm, shaping how we express ourselves and how we channel our energy into the world.

Celebrating Inner Rhythm

To embrace passion is to celebrate the unique rhythm of energy within you. It is a call to listen to your inner voice, to honor the moments that shape you, and to express yourself fully and authentically. Whether through movement, art, or words, passion is the rhythm that makes life vibrant, meaningful, and extraordinary.

Passion, like rhythm, is a dance of energy—a dance that only you can choreograph. By tuning into your rhythm and expressing it in your own way, you create a life that resonates with purpose, joy, and connection.

Design and Language as Expressions

Design and language are profound forms of expression, each with the unique ability to shape perception, convey meaning, and connect the present to the future. They are not merely tools of communication but also vehicles for creativity, intention, and transformation. Together, they embody the essence of human expression, providing a bridge between thought and reality, self and others, and today and tomorrow.

Design: The Visual Language of Intention

Design is more than aesthetics; it is the visual language of intention. Every element of design—whether in architecture, technology, fashion, or art—carries meaning. It transforms abstract thoughts into tangible realities, giving form to ideas and structure to imagination.

A well-crafted design tells a story. It communicates purpose, evokes emotion, and influences behavior. Consider a building: its design reflects the architect's vision, the functionality it serves, and the cultural or historical context it inhabits. Similarly, a product's design not only determines its usability but also speaks to the values and priorities of its creator.

In this way, design becomes an extension of the designer's inner world. It is an expression of creativity, a manifestation of problem-solving, and a dialogue between intention and execution.

Language: The Articulation of Identity and Aspiration

Language, like design, is an expression of identity and aspiration. It is the articulation of who you are and who you wish to become. Through language, humans convey their deepest thoughts, share their experiences, and connect with one another.

Language has the power to shape reality. The words you choose and the way you express them influence not only how others perceive you but also how you perceive yourself. When you articulate your goals, dreams, and values, you are creating a blueprint for your future self. Language, in this sense, is a tool for self-transformation, a means of aligning your present actions with your future aspirations.

Expression: Connecting Present to Future

Expression is the thread that connects the present to the future. It is how you communicate with your future self, shaping your destiny through the words and actions of today. Every expression—whether through design, language, or other mediums—carries intention and energy.

When you express gratitude, for instance, you reinforce a positive outlook, creating a foundation for future joy and abundance. When you articulate your goals, you set the stage for action, turning abstract dreams into achievable milestones. Expression, therefore, is not just a reflection of the present but also a powerful tool for shaping the future.

The Purpose of Language

Language is a gift, and its highest purpose is to serve the virtues of humanity. It is a tool that can uplift, inspire, and transform when used with intention and alignment to universal values.

1. **Appreciation** Language allows us to honor the beauty and efforts of life. Through words of appreciation, we acknowledge the value of what surrounds us—the people, the environment, and the experiences that shape us. Appreciation is a form of recognition that fosters connection and mutual respect.

2. **Generosity** in language is about sharing openly—ideas, knowledge, and kindness. When we use words to uplift others, we spread positivity and inspire connection. Such communication brings people together and bridges differences.

3. **Gratitude** is the acknowledgment of what has been given. Through language, we express our thanks for life's blessings, both big and small. Gratitude transforms our perspective, shifting focus from scarcity to abundance, and deepening our connection to others and the divine.

Design and Language: A Synergistic Relationship

Design and language often work together, amplifying each other's impact. A well-designed piece of writing, for example, uses both visual and linguistic elements to convey its message effectively. Similarly, a design project may rely on language to articulate its purpose, guiding its audience toward understanding and appreciation.

In branding, this synergy is especially evident. The design of a logo, the choice of colors, and the typography all contribute to a brand's identity. At the same time, the language of the brand—its tagline, mission statement, and tone—shapes how it is perceived. Together, design and language create a cohesive narrative, expressing the essence of the brand.

Expression as Transformation

When aligned with virtues like appreciation, generosity, and gratitude, both design and language become forces of transformation. They move beyond mere functionality, becoming tools for creating meaning, fostering connection, and inspiring change.

Expression through design can transform spaces, making them more inclusive, inspiring, or functional. A thoughtfully designed public park, for example, becomes a place of community and joy. Similarly, language can transform relationships, fostering understanding, healing, and growth.

On a personal level, expression is how we evolve. By consciously choosing how we express ourselves—through the words we speak, the designs we create, or the actions we take—we shape our identity and influence our path.

Expression as Divine Connection

At its highest level, expression connects us to the divine essence within ourselves and others. When language and design are used to honor virtues, they become more than tools; they become sacred acts. They remind us of our interconnectedness and our shared humanity.

Expression, in this sense, is a spiritual practice. It is how we honor the life force within us, how we connect with others, and how we contribute to the world. When we express ourselves with intention and authenticity, we align with our higher purpose, creating a legacy of meaning and impact.

"Expression is the soul's bridge to the world—where energy becomes action, thoughts become reality, and the rhythm of passion shapes the future we dare to dream."

CHAPTER 3: "THE INNER SYMPHONY: UNDERSTANDING AND HARMONIZING THOUGHTS AND EMOTIONS"

3.1: The Observer Within

Our inner world is like a vibrant landscape, constantly shifting with feelings and thoughts. These emotions and ideas come and go, much like visitors passing through a bustling city. As the observer, we have the unique ability to welcome these thoughts and feelings, understand them, and decide how we want to engage with them. This chapter invites you to explore the practice of observing your inner world without judgment, fostering a deeper, more harmonious connection with yourself.

3.1.1: Observing Feelings and Thoughts

Feelings and thoughts are temporary—they come and go like waves on the ocean. When we take on the role of the observer, we create space to see them clearly without becoming overwhelmed by them. This doesn't mean ignoring or pushing away our emotions; it means acknowledging them with curiosity and compassion.

Imagine standing beside a river, watching the water flow. The river represents your emotions and thoughts, constantly moving, never stagnant. As the observer, you don't get swept away by the current. Instead, you stand firm, watching the water pass by. This perspective helps you realize that emotions like anger, joy, or sadness are temporary—they don't define who you are. They're just part of your experience.

Observing your thoughts requires mindfulness—the ability to be fully present without judgment. Through practices like meditation or journaling, you can strengthen this skill. For example, when anger arises, instead of reacting right away, pause and ask yourself: "What triggered this emotion? What can I learn from it?" This simple act of reflection deepens your understanding of your inner world and empowers you to respond thoughtfully.

3.1.2: Reacting with Peace, Acceptance, and Kindness

How we respond to our emotions shapes our inner peace. By choosing peace, acceptance, and kindness as our natural responses, we create a nurturing environment within ourselves.

Peace doesn't mean there's no chaos; it means staying steady within, even when the world around us feels turbulent. For instance, if work stress overwhelms you, instead of letting frustration take over, take a deep breath and remind yourself that this moment, like all others, will pass. This grounding moment brings calm amidst the storm.

Acceptance means allowing your emotions to be what they are without fighting them. It's about sitting with discomfort and recognizing it as a natural part of life. When sadness arises, instead of avoiding it, say to yourself, "It's okay to feel this way. This too shall pass." Acceptance doesn't mean giving up; it means embracing the moment, which paradoxically gives you the strength to move through it.

Kindness is the healing balm for the soul. When negative thoughts arise, meet them with compassion. Replace harsh self-criticism with supportive words. For example, if you make a mistake, instead of beating yourself up, say, "I'm human, and it's okay to make mistakes. What can I learn from this?" Kindness nurtures resilience and strengthens your bond with yourself.

3.1.3: The Power of Smiling Through Uncomfortable Feelings

Smiling is a powerful act of self-empowerment, even in the face of discomfort. It's not about forcing happiness but about telling yourself that you have the strength to endure and grow through challenges.

Think about a difficult moment you've faced—maybe a disagreement or a setback at work. In these moments, smiling may seem unnatural, but it can shift your mindset. A smile, even a small one, releases endorphins, the body's natural "feel-good" chemicals. This small gesture doesn't make the discomfort go away, but it offers a brief respite, a reminder that you are more than your struggles.

Smiling through pain also opens your heart to gratitude. It's a way of acknowledging that joy and sorrow are two sides of the same coin. It's like dancing in the rain, accepting the storm rather than waiting for it to end. This simple act of self-acceptance turns adversity into strength.

3.1.4: Realizing You Are More Than Your Feelings

At the core of this practice lies a profound truth: you are more than your feelings. Emotions are fleeting—they rise and fall like waves, but beneath them lies your true self, steady and constant, like the ocean beneath the surface.

This realization is freeing. When we identify only with our emotions, we risk being swept away by them. For example, if you feel angry, you might think, "I am an angry person." But by observing the emotion, you can shift your perspective and say, "I am experiencing anger." This small shift helps you realize that you are not your emotions. You are the one who witnesses them.

This understanding empowers you to navigate life with greater clarity. You can honor your emotions without being overwhelmed by them. For example, when anxiety arises before a big presentation, instead of saying, "I am anxious," say, "Anxiety is present." This simple reframe creates space between you and the emotion, allowing you to respond with calm and confidence.

Realizing you are more than your feelings opens the door to personal growth. It encourages you to explore the deeper parts of yourself—your values, passions, and purpose. You become less reactive and more intentional, less ruled by fleeting emotions and more aligned with your true self.

Embracing the Observer Within

As you cultivate the observer within, you tap into a well of inner peace and strength. You learn to dance with your emotions, honoring them as essential parts of your experience without letting them define you. This practice transforms challenges into opportunities, leading you to a life of greater harmony and fulfillment.

So, take a moment to pause and observe. Welcome your feelings and thoughts as visitors, treat them with peace, acceptance, and kindness. Smile through discomfort, knowing it's part of the dance of life. And most importantly, remember: you are more than your feelings. You are the observer, the vast ocean beneath the waves, and there is great power in that.

3.2: Understanding Feelings

Feelings are the silent poetry of the soul, an intricate and perpetual dance between the heart's raw emotions and the mind's thoughtful musings. They serve as the invisible threads weaving together the tapestry of our lives, giving color and meaning to every experience, every fleeting moment, and every enduring connection.

Just as the ocean ebbs and flows with currents both gentle and fierce, our feelings move through us, sometimes as tranquil as a whispering breeze, other times as overwhelming as a tempest. They are at once a reflection of our innermost selves and a response to the world around us. To truly understand who we are, to comprehend our unique place in the cosmos, we must embark on the profound journey of understanding our feelings.

This chapter is an invitation to that journey—an inward exploration of the origins, nuances, and transformative power of our emotions. It is an opportunity to delve deeper into the symphony of feelings that shape our lives, to learn how to listen to them, interpret their meaning, and embrace their guidance.

The Language of Feelings

Feelings are not random or accidental; they are purposeful signals, messengers from within, carrying the wisdom of the subconscious.

When we learn to decipher this language, we unlock the potential to navigate life with greater clarity and intention.

Imagine a world without feelings—every joy flattened, every sorrow muted, every connection devoid of depth. It is our feelings that breathe life into our experiences, transforming mundane moments into memories and ordinary interactions into profound relationships. They are the bridge between what we think and what we truly know, the compass that guides us through the complexities of existence.

Why Understanding Feelings Matters

1. **Self-Awareness:** To understand our feelings is to understand ourselves. Emotions reveal what we value, what we fear, and what we hope for. They are a mirror reflecting our deepest truths.

2. **Better Relationships:** When we recognize and honor our own feelings, we become better equipped to empathize with others. This understanding fosters deeper, more meaningful connections.

3. **Resilience and Growth:** Feelings, especially the challenging ones, are opportunities for growth. They teach us patience, courage, and the strength to overcome life's adversities.

4. **Authentic Living:** By tuning into our emotions, we align our actions with our values, leading to a life of authenticity and purpose.

The Spectrum of Feelings

Feelings exist on a vast spectrum, from the fleeting sparks of joy to the heavy shadows of despair. Each feeling has its own story to tell, its own lesson to impart.

- **Positive Feelings:** These are the emotions that uplift and energize us, such as love, gratitude, and excitement. They remind us of life's beauty and inspire us to dream bigger and live fuller.

- **Neutral Feelings:** Often overlooked, neutral feelings like calmness or contentment are the steady anchors in the storms of life. They ground us, offering a sense of balance and peace.
- **Negative Feelings:** Though uncomfortable, emotions like anger, fear, and sadness are essential for growth. They alert us to challenges, motivate us to act, and teach us resilience.

Every feeling, whether joyful, calm, or painful, has a purpose in our emotional world. Together, they weave the complex and beautiful experience of being human.

Feelings as a Journey, Not a Destination

Understanding feelings is not about achieving perpetual happiness or eliminating negative emotions. Instead, it is about embracing the full spectrum of human experience. Life is a journey of peaks and valleys, and our emotions are the map guiding us through it.

- **The Peaks:** Moments of joy, love, and success are the peaks of our emotional journey. They are reminders of what is possible, encouraging us to keep climbing.
- **The Valleys:** Pain, loss, and fear are the valleys where we grow. These moments challenge us to reflect, adapt, and find new strength.

By seeing feelings as part of a journey rather than a destination, we learn to appreciate every moment for what it is—a step forward in our personal evolution.

Practical Steps to Understanding Feelings

1. **Acknowledge Your Emotions:** The first step to understanding feelings is to acknowledge their presence. Instead of suppressing or ignoring your emotions, take a moment to name them.

   Example: If you feel overwhelmed, pause and say, "I am feeling overwhelmed right now." Naming your emotions reduces their intensity and gives you a sense of control.

2. **Reflect on Their Origins:** Every feeling has a trigger. Reflect on what caused your emotion. Was it an external event, a memory, or an expectation?

   Example: If you feel angry, ask yourself, "What triggered this anger? Is it about the situation, or is it connected to something deeper?"

3. **Observe Without Judgment:** Treat your feelings as visitors. Observe them without labeling them as good or bad.

   Exercise: Practice mindfulness by sitting quietly and noticing your emotions. Imagine them as clouds passing through the sky of your mind.

4. **Express Your Emotions:** Bottling up feelings can lead to emotional distress. Find healthy ways to express your emotions, such as journaling, talking to a trusted friend, or engaging in creative activities.

5. **Learn from Your Emotions:** Every feeling carries a message. Ask yourself, "What is this emotion trying to teach me?" Use this insight to make informed decisions and grow as a person.

3.2.1: Emotional States

At the heart of every feeling lies an emotional state—a nuanced and dynamic response to the ever-changing world within and around us. These states are as diverse as the hues of a sunset, each offering its own lens through which we perceive and experience life. Emotional states are not merely reactions; they are the soul's way of painting meaning onto the canvas of existence.

Let us delve deeper into some of the most profound emotional states, exploring their essence and their power to shape our connections, growth, and humanity.

Love, Care, Affection, Tenderness

These emotions are the foundation of human connection—the invisible threads that weave us into each other's lives. Love transcends the boundaries of time and space; it is not merely an emotion but a boundless energy. Manifesting as care in action, affection in words, and tenderness in touch, love is the heartbeat of all meaningful relationships.

Reflection:

Think of the last time you truly felt loved. Was it in the warmth of a comforting embrace, the melody of a kind word, or the quiet beauty of a selfless act? Love, when nurtured, becomes the fertile soil where relationships bloom and flourish.

Love whispers in the quiet moments, radiates in acts of care, and echoes in the smallest gestures—a reassuring smile, a hand extended in support, or the unspoken understanding of someone who sees your soul.

Perspective:

Love is the seed, care is the nurturing rain, affection is the sunlight, and tenderness is the soft earth in which the roots of connection grow deep.

Compassion, Empathy, Sympathy

These emotions are a testament to our shared humanity, the bonds that remind us we are never alone in our joys or our struggles.

- **Compassion** is the gentle yearning to ease another's suffering.

- **Empathy** is the ability to step into their shoes, feeling their emotions as if they were your own.
- **Sympathy** is the acknowledgment of another's pain, offering comfort and solidarity.

Analogy:

Compassion is like a soft, nourishing rain that refreshes the weary. Empathy is the flowing river, connecting one heart to another in a seamless current of understanding. Sympathy is the sturdy bridge, a gesture of kindness that spans the gap between isolation and connection.

Analogy:

Compassion is like a soft, nourishing rain that refreshes the weary. Empathy is the flowing river, connecting one heart to another in a seamless current of understanding. Sympathy is the sturdy bridge, a gesture of kindness that spans the gap between isolation and connection.

Reflection:

When was the last time you felt truly connected to someone else's emotions? Perhaps it was through the quiet understanding of a friend's grief, the unspoken solidarity in a shared challenge, or the active effort to bring light to someone's darkness.

Compassion, empathy, and sympathy are not weaknesses but strengths—they transform relationships and heal wounds that words alone cannot.

Sorrow, Pity, Condolences

In the intricate tapestry of life, sorrow is the thread that reminds us of life's fragility and fleeting beauty. It humbles us, teaches us gratitude, and urges us to live fully in the present moment.

- **Sorrow** allows us to honor what we have lost and what we hold dear.

- **Pity** is the recognition of another's suffering, tempered by the understanding of their humanity.
- **Condolences** are the expressions of solidarity, an acknowledgment that no one should bear the weight of grief alone.

Reflection:

How do you honor your sorrows? Do you bury them beneath the weight of distraction, or do you allow them to guide you toward understanding, resilience, and growth?

Sorrow, when embraced, becomes a teacher—a mirror reflecting the depth of our love and the preciousness of life itself.

Perspective:

Sorrow is not a void but a vessel. It carries us through the storm, reminding us of our capacity to endure and the profound beauty of what it means to feel deeply.

3.2.2: Ideas and Beliefs as Feelings

Feelings are not always rooted in raw emotion; they often originate from the intricate web of our thoughts, beliefs, and perceptions. These are the quiet whispers of the subconscious, subtle signals that illuminate the path of our intuition and influence the decisions we make every day. They form the bridge between the mind and the heart, weaving together logic and instinct to shape how we perceive and respond to the world around us.

Suspicion, Notion, Hunch, Sixth Sense

These feelings emerge from the depths of our inner wisdom, often defying the boundaries of logic and rationality. They are the quiet murmurs of experience, the echoes of lessons learned, and the unspoken truths stored deep within our psyche.

- **Suspicion** arises as a cautious guardian, urging us to tread carefully when something feels amiss.
- **Notion** is the seed of an idea, a fleeting thought that plants itself in our consciousness, waiting to grow.
- **Hunch** is the intuitive nudge, a whisper from within that tells us to trust what we cannot yet see.
- **Sixth Sense** transcends explanation, a visceral awareness that often feels like a gift from beyond logic—a mysterious force guiding us toward clarity.

These sensations are not random; they are informed by a tapestry of past experiences, knowledge, and subtle observations. They are the subconscious mind's way of processing information too complex or too nuanced for the conscious mind to fully grasp.

Reflection

How often do you pause to trust your instincts? In a world dominated by logic and data, it is easy to dismiss these subtle cues as irrational or unfounded. Yet, they are often the voice of your subconscious, urging you to pay attention to something your conscious mind might overlook.

The next time you have a hunch or a gut feeling, resist the urge to dismiss it outright. Instead, pause and listen. What is it trying to tell you? Is it drawing your attention to something you might have missed? Or is it cautioning you against a path that might not serve your best interests?

The Power of Inner Wisdom

- **Suspicion:** Imagine standing at a crossroads, faced with a choice that seems perfect on the surface but feels unsettling. Suspicion is your mind's way of urging you to look deeper, to question what lies beneath the facade.

- **Notion:** Picture a fleeting thought—an idea that sparks curiosity or inspiration. A notion is often the birthplace of innovation, a tiny spark that, when nurtured, can grow into something transformative.
- **Hunch:** Recall a moment when you "just knew" something without evidence. That gut feeling often arises from a culmination of past experiences and subtle cues your mind has picked up on, even if you are not consciously aware of them.
- **Sixth Sense:** Consider the inexplicable feeling of being watched or the sense of knowing something before it happens. The sixth sense is a reminder of the profound connection between our intuition and the universe.

Practical Application

1. **Acknowledge:** When you feel a hunch or an instinct, don't ignore it. Acknowledge its presence, even if it feels irrational at first.
2. **Reflect:** Ask yourself why this feeling might have arisen. What past experiences or observations could be informing it?
3. **Act with Balance:** Use these feelings as guides, not as sole decision-makers. Combine them with logic and reason for a well-rounded perspective.

3.2.3: Instant vs. Time-Taking Feelings

The spectrum of human emotion is vast, encompassing feelings that burst forth like shooting stars and others that unfold like the slow bloom of a flower. Both types play distinct and vital roles in shaping our emotional landscape, offering lessons and insights that guide us through life.

Instant Feelings

Instant feelings are the emotional sparks that ignite in a moment, quick to flare and just as quick to fade. They often arise in response to external stimuli—situations, interactions, or sudden realizations. These emotions are fleeting but powerful, capable of influencing our actions and decisions in an instant.

- **Anger:** A fiery response to perceived injustice or frustration. It's a natural reaction to situations where boundaries are crossed or expectations are unmet.
- **Envy:** A shadow of longing that emerges when we see someone achieve or possess something we desire. It often reflects our deeper aspirations or insecurities.
- **Regret:** A sharp pang of disappointment or sorrow when reflecting on a past mistake or missed opportunity. It reminds us of our imperfections and the lessons we still need to learn.
- **Ego:** A defensive shield we raise to protect our self-image, often triggered when we feel criticized, overlooked, or undervalued.

Reflection on Instant Feelings

Instant feelings are like fireflies—brief flashes of light that capture our attention but are not meant to last. While they demand our focus in the moment, they are transient and often fade as quickly as they arise.

- **Observe Without Attachment:** Instant feelings can overwhelm us if we cling to them or act impulsively. Instead, observe them as passing visitors, acknowledging their presence without letting them take control.
- **Pause Before Reacting:** The next time you feel a surge of anger or envy, pause. Take a deep breath and ask yourself: What is this emotion trying to tell me? What action, if any, is truly necessary?
- **Learn From the Spark:** Each instant feeling carries a message. Anger may signal a need for boundaries, while regret can illuminate areas for growth. Use these sparks as tools for self-awareness.

Time-Taking Feelings

In contrast to the fleeting nature of instant feelings, time-taking feelings are those that settle deep within us, growing richer and more profound over time.

They are the steady undercurrents of our emotional world, requiring nurturing, patience, and intentionality to fully manifest.

- **Joy:** A radiant glow that comes from living authentically and in alignment with your values. It is not merely a fleeting moment of happiness but a sustained sense of fulfillment.
- **Peace:** The quiet strength that arises from acceptance, understanding, and letting go of control. Peace is a deep well of calm that sustains us even in turbulent times.
- **Kindness:** The gentle ripple effect of compassion in action. It is a long-term practice of empathy and generosity that builds meaningful connections.
- **Generosity:** The enduring fulfillment of giving without expectation. True generosity grows with time, as we see its impact on others and feel its warmth in our hearts.

Reflection on Time-Taking Feelings

Time-taking feelings are like trees—slow to grow but deeply rooted, offering shade and sustenance as they mature.

- **Cultivate With Care:** Just as a tree requires sunlight, water, and soil to thrive, time-taking feelings need consistent attention. Joy, peace, kindness, and generosity are cultivated through daily choices and intentional actions.
- **Celebrate Their Depth:** Unlike instant feelings, time-taking emotions are not about intensity but depth. Celebrate the quiet, enduring glow of joy or the steady comfort of peace as gifts that enrich your life.
- **Share Their Fruits:** Time-taking feelings often overflow, benefiting not just the individual but also those around them. Kindness inspires kindness, and generosity sparks gratitude.

The Balance Between Instant and Time-Taking Feelings

Both types of feelings are essential. Instant feelings keep us present and reactive to the world, helping us navigate challenges and opportunities in real-time. Time-taking feelings, on the other hand, provide stability, meaning, and purpose, grounding us in the bigger picture of life.

- **Embrace Both:** Allow yourself to experience the full spectrum of emotions, from the fleeting sparks to the enduring currents. Each has its place and purpose.
- **Respond, Don't React:** With instant feelings, focus on response over reaction. With time-taking feelings, focus on nurturing them consistently.
- **Reflect and Grow:** Use instant feelings as lessons and time-taking feelings as milestones. Together, they chart the journey of your emotional growth.

The Science of Feelings

Feelings are not merely abstract, intangible experiences; they are deeply rooted in the intricate workings of our biology and psychology. Modern neuroscience and psychology provide profound insights into how feelings emerge, how they shape our lives, and how we can harness their power for growth and well-being.

The Limbic System: The Emotional Brain

At the heart of our emotional experiences lies the limbic system, often referred to as the "emotional brain." This network of interconnected structures in the brain, including the amygdala, hippocampus, and hypothalamus, is responsible for processing emotions, forming memories, and regulating bodily responses.

- **Amygdala:** Known as the brain's alarm system, the amygdala plays a critical role in detecting threats and triggering the "fight or flight" response. It processes emotions like fear, anger, and pleasure, often initiating immediate reactions to stimuli.

- **Hippocampus:** This structure is essential for encoding emotional memories. It helps contextualize feelings by associating them with past experiences, enabling us to learn from our emotional history.
- **Hypothalamus:** The hypothalamus links emotions to physical responses, such as increased heart rate during fear or a sense of calm during relaxation.

The Prefrontal Cortex: The Seat of Regulation

While the limbic system generates emotions, the prefrontal cortex—located at the front of the brain—helps us regulate and respond to them. This region is responsible for higher-order functions like decision-making, impulse control, and emotional regulation.

- **Mindfulness and Emotional Regulation:** When we practice mindfulness, we activate the prefrontal cortex, creating a "pause button" between stimulus and response. This allows us to consciously choose our reactions instead of being driven by impulsive emotional responses from the amygdala.
- **Cognitive Reappraisal:** Research shows that engaging the prefrontal cortex enables cognitive reappraisal—rethinking a situation to change its emotional impact. For instance, reframing a failure as a learning opportunity reduces feelings of regret and boosts resilience.

Neurochemical Foundations of Feelings

Feelings are also influenced by a complex interplay of neurochemicals in the brain:

- **Dopamine:** Often called the "feel-good" neurotransmitter, dopamine is associated with reward, motivation, and pleasure. It plays a key role in feelings of joy and satisfaction.
- **Serotonin:** This neurotransmitter contributes to feelings of well-being and happiness. Low serotonin levels are linked to depression and anxiety.

- **Oxytocin:** Known as the "love hormone," oxytocin fosters bonding, trust, and connection in relationships.
- **Cortisol:** This stress hormone is released during moments of fear or anxiety. Chronic high levels of cortisol can negatively impact emotional health.

The Role of Mirror Neurons

Mirror neurons, a special class of neurons discovered in the 1990s, are key players in empathy and social connection. These neurons fire both when we perform an action and when we observe someone else performing the same action, allowing us to "mirror" their feelings.

- **Empathy in Action:** When we see someone smile, our mirror neurons activate, creating a similar feeling of happiness within us. This mechanism underpins our ability to empathize and connect with others on an emotional level.

Psychological Perspectives on Feelings

From a psychological standpoint, feelings are shaped by both nature and nurture:

- **Evolutionary Psychology:** Emotions evolved as survival mechanisms. Fear kept our ancestors safe from predators, while joy reinforced behaviors that promoted bonding and cooperation.
- **Cognitive-Behavioral Theory:** This theory posits that our feelings are influenced by our thoughts and beliefs. For example, interpreting a challenging situation as an opportunity rather than a threat can transform anxiety into excitement.
- **Attachment Theory:** Developed by John Bowlby, this theory highlights the importance of early relationships in shaping our emotional patterns. Secure attachments in childhood lead to healthier emotional regulation in adulthood.

The Interplay Between Feelings and the Body

Feelings are not confined to the brain; they manifest throughout the body in ways that influence our physical health:

- **The Gut-Brain Axis:** The gut is often referred to as the "second brain" because it contains millions of neurons and produces 90% of the body's serotonin. The gut-brain connection explains why stress can lead to digestive issues and why a healthy diet supports emotional well-being.
- **Somatic Responses:** Emotions are felt physically—tightness in the chest during anxiety, warmth in the heart during love, or a sinking feeling in the stomach during disappointment. These bodily sensations are integral to the experience of feelings.

The Power of Mindfulness and Emotional Mastery

Neuroscience confirms that we can train our brains to better understand and manage feelings:

- **Neuroplasticity:** The brain's ability to reorganize itself means that consistent practices like mindfulness, gratitude, and journaling can strengthen the neural pathways associated with positive emotions.
- **Mindfulness Meditation:** Studies show that mindfulness reduces activity in the amygdala and increases connectivity between the amygdala and prefrontal cortex, enhancing emotional regulation.
- **Gratitude Practices:** Regularly focusing on what we are thankful for boosts dopamine and serotonin levels, fostering a lasting sense of well-being.

3.3.1: Physical Body & Mental Mind

The connection between our physical body and mental mind has been a topic of deep discussion in philosophy for centuries. This section explores different ideas about how the two are related.

Dualism (Mind-Body Problem):

Descartes' Dualism: One of the most famous views on this topic comes from René Descartes. He believed that the mind and body are two separate entities. The body is made of matter and functions in the physical world, while the mind (or soul) is non-physical and exists in a different realm. The big question this raises is: How can something that isn't physical (like thoughts or emotions) influence the physical body?

Monism (Mind and Body as One):

Materialism: Materialism suggests that the mind and body are not separate. Instead, the mind is a product of the physical processes in our brain. According to this view, everything we think and feel is connected to brain activity.

Idealism: On the other side, idealism proposes that reality is fundamentally mental or spiritual. In this view, the body might just be a reflection of the mind, not an independent entity.

Embodiment and the Mind-Body Connection:

Phenomenology: Philosophers like Maurice Merleau-Ponty argued that the mind and body are so deeply connected that they can't be understood separately. Our experiences, thoughts, and feelings are rooted in our physical bodies, meaning the way we interact with the world is shaped by our physical existence.

Mindfulness and Presence: In modern times, mindfulness practices emphasize the connection between mind and body. For example, physical activities like exercise can improve our mood, and mental stress can lead to physical problems like headaches or back pain. This highlights the two-way relationship between our body and mind.

Ethics and the Mind-Body Relationship:

The mind-body connection also raises ethical questions. For instance, what are our responsibilities when it comes to caring for both our physical and mental health? How does the state of our body affect our mental abilities and moral decisions? This relationship plays a crucial role in our overall well-being and how we navigate life.

CHAPTER 4: ABRAHAM MASLOW'S HIERARCHY OF NEEDS AND FEAR

Abraham Maslow's Hierarchy of Needs

In the rich tapestry of human thought, Abraham Maslow's Hierarchy of Needs emerges as a philosophical cornerstone, a guiding light for those seeking to unravel the intricate threads of human motivation. Introduced in his 1943 paper, "A Theory of Human Motivation," this framework does more than categorize needs; it offers a profound reflection on the human condition, a roadmap to our deepest aspirations. Maslow's pyramid, with its layered progression from the tangible to the transcendent, invites us to contemplate not just what we need, but who we are.

The Five Tiers of Maslow's Hierarchy

1. Physiological Needs

At the foundation of existence lies the undeniable truth of our physicality. Physiological needs are the anchors of survival, the unspoken contract between body and soul. They remind us of the raw simplicity of being alive:

- **Food and Water:** The elemental sustenance that binds us to the earth.
- **Air:** The quiet, rhythmic breath that whispers life into our lungs.
- **Shelter:** A sanctuary against the chaos of the natural world.
- **Sleep:** The restorative embrace of night.
- **Clothing:** A shield, a statement, a necessity.

In these needs, we find the poetry of survival, a dance between fragility and resilience. Without these foundations, the higher pursuits of the spirit remain elusive.

2. Safety Needs

When the body is sated, the heart turns to security. Safety needs are not merely about the absence of danger but the presence of peace—a sense that the world can be navigated without fear:

- **Physical Safety:** A haven from harm, a place to stand firm.
- **Health and Well-being:** The vitality that allows us to face each day.
- **Financial Security:** Stability that fosters hope and possibility.
- **Predictability:** The gentle rhythm of order in a chaotic world.

Here lies the quiet yearning for stability, a shield against the unpredictable currents of existence.

3. Love and Belongingness Needs

The third tier beckons us to the realm of connection, where the solitary self seeks communion with others. Love and belongingness are the threads that weave us into the fabric of humanity:

- **Relationships:** The touch of friendship, the warmth of kinship.
- **Community:** A circle where we find acceptance and identity.
- **Affection and Acceptance:** The sacred validation that reminds us we are seen, we are known.

These needs speak to the soul's hunger for intimacy and understanding. To belong is to affirm our place in the grand mosaic of life.

4. Esteem Needs

As connections deepen, the individual seeks affirmation—not just from others but from within. Esteem needs are the twin flames of recognition and self-respect:

- **Self-Esteem:** The quiet pride of competence and independence.
- **Recognition from Others:** The applause, the acknowledgment, the shared triumph.

Esteem elevates us, urging us to stand tall in our own eyes and in the eyes of the world. It is the architecture of dignity, the scaffolding of ambition.

5. Self-Actualization Needs

At the pyramid's peak lies self-actualization, the sacred quest to become one's fullest self. This is not a destination but a journey, an unfolding of potential:

- **Personal Growth:** The ceaseless pursuit of wisdom and creativity.
- **Purpose and Meaning:** A life lived in alignment with one's deepest values.
- **Peak Experiences:** Those fleeting moments when the ordinary becomes extraordinary, when we touch the infinite.

Self-actualization is the art of being, the poetry of becoming. It is the call to transcend the mundane and embrace the sublime.

Key Principles of Maslow's Theory

1. Sequential Fulfillment

Maslow's hierarchy suggests a natural progression, yet life often defies neat categories. While basic needs demand attention, the human spirit may reach for higher realms even in the face of adversity.

2. Deficiency vs. Growth Needs

The distinction between deficiency and growth needs captures the dual nature of human striving. Deficiency needs call out in their absence, urging us to fill voids. Growth needs, however, are the whispers of possibility, the pull toward expansion and transcendence.

3. Cultural and Individual Variations

Maslow's hierarchy is not a one-size-fits-all map. Cultures and individuals navigate these needs in unique ways, shaped by history, values, and personal journeys. What binds us is the shared yearning to climb, to aspire, to be.

Applications of Maslow's Hierarchy

1. Education

Education is the alchemy of potential into reality. By addressing Maslow's hierarchy, educators nurture the whole person:

- Meeting physiological needs ensures students are ready to learn.
- Creating a safe and inclusive environment fosters security and belonging.
- Recognizing achievements builds esteem.
- Encouraging curiosity and creativity opens the door to self-actualization.

2. Workplace Motivation

In the workplace, Maslow's hierarchy becomes a blueprint for engagement:

- Fair wages and safe conditions honor basic needs.
- A culture of respect and camaraderie fulfills social aspirations.
- Recognition & growth opportunities ignite the flame of self-actualization.

3. Healthcare and Therapy

In healing professions, Maslow's insights guide a holistic approach:

- Addressing physical ailments lays the groundwork for recovery.
- Emotional support and a sense of safety nurture the spirit.
- Empowering patients fosters dignity and hope.

4. Marketing and Consumer Behavior

Marketers tap into the hierarchy to resonate with human desires:

- Basic products promise survival and comfort.
- Social platforms connect and affirm.
- Aspirational brands invite us to dream.

Criticisms and Limitations

Maslow's theory, like all great ideas, is not without its critics. Some question its empirical foundation, others its cultural biases. Life's complexity often defies linear models, as needs intertwine and overlap. Yet, the essence of the hierarchy—its invitation to explore the layers of human motivation—remains undiminished.

Evolving Perspectives

In his later work, Maslow expanded his vision, adding layers of cognitive and aesthetic needs, even transcendence—the urge to lift others toward their own self-actualization. These additions reflect the boundless nature of human aspiration.

4.1.1: Physiological Needs – Food, Water, Shelter

Physiological needs are the foundation of Maslow's hierarchy, encompassing the most basic requirements for human survival. These include food, water, shelter, and other necessities such as sleep and air. Without these, individuals cannot function effectively. Food provides the energy required for bodily functions, while water is essential for hydration and metabolic processes. Shelter offers protection from environmental hazards and contributes to physical security.

For instance, consider a person living in poverty who struggles to access clean water or adequate nutrition. Such deprivation dominates their focus, leaving little room for concerns beyond immediate survival. This highlights the critical role of physiological needs in shaping human behavior and priorities. Societies with stable access to these essentials tend to exhibit higher levels of development and innovation, as their populations can concentrate on advanced pursuits.

4.1.2: Safety and Security – Freedom from Fear

Once physiological needs are met, the next priority becomes safety and security. This category includes physical safety, financial stability, health, and protection from harm. Humans have an innate desire to live in environments free from danger, chaos, and uncertainty.

Safety extends beyond physical well-being to encompass emotional and psychological aspects. For example, a stable job provides financial security, while a safe community fosters a sense of peace. Conversely, living in a conflict zone or facing financial instability triggers chronic stress and anxiety, which can hinder personal growth.

Freedom from fear is a cornerstone of this level. Fear—whether stemming from violence, economic uncertainty, or health crises—can paralyze individuals and communities. In today's context, the COVID-19 pandemic exemplifies the disruption caused when safety needs are threatened. People worldwide experienced heightened anxiety as their health and economic security were jeopardized. Governments and organizations responded by implementing measures to restore safety, emphasizing its foundational importance in Maslow's framework.

Maslow's theory suggests that achieving safety and security allows individuals to shift their focus toward higher-order needs. For instance, a person who feels secure in their home and job is more likely to invest time and energy into building relationships or pursuing personal goals. However, safety remains a dynamic need, influenced by external factors such as political stability, economic conditions, and social infrastructure. Addressing these variables is crucial for fostering environments where individuals can thrive.

4.1.3: Belonging and Love – Friends, Family, Community

At the heart of human experience lies the profound need for connection—a yearning to belong, to be seen, and to be loved. In Maslow's Hierarchy of Needs, the third tier, **Belonging and Love,** encapsulates this deep-seated desire. Positioned above the foundational layers of physiological and safety needs, this level represents our innate drive to form meaningful relationships and immerse ourselves in communities that affirm our identity and purpose. It is through this lens that we explore the transformative power of friends, family, and community in fulfilling this vital human need.

The Essence of Belonging

Belonging is more than a social construct; it is a cornerstone of emotional and psychological well-being. The human spirit craves acceptance and connection, as these foster a sense of security and identity. To belong is to feel rooted, to know that one has a place in the intricate web of relationships that define our existence. Without this, the human psyche can experience loneliness, isolation, and a sense of fragmentation.

This tier is not simply about forming any relationships, but about cultivating **meaningful bonds** that enrich and support our journey through life. It speaks to the depth of connection, encompassing:

- **Friendship:** Bonds formed through shared experiences, trust, and mutual understanding.
- **Family:** The unconditional support and love from those tied by blood or deep emotional ties.
- **Community:** A collective sense of belonging through shared values, culture, and purpose.

Friendship: The Chosen Family

Friendship occupies a sacred space in the realm of belonging. Unlike familial ties, which are often predetermined, friendships are chosen and nurtured. They are relationships built on:

- **Trust:** The foundation of any meaningful connection, trust enables vulnerability and openness.
- **Shared Experiences:** Moments of joy, challenge, and growth that strengthen the bond.
- **Mutual Support:** The give-and-take of care, advice, and encouragement.

Friendships are vital in shaping our identity and worldview. They provide a mirror to our inner selves, offering feedback, validation, and the opportunity to grow. In times of distress, a friend's presence can be a balm, while in moments of triumph, their celebration amplifies joy.

Modern psychology underscores the importance of friendships in promoting mental health. Research reveals that strong social ties can reduce stress, increase happiness, and even enhance longevity. In the digital age, while virtual connections have expanded the scope of friendships, the essence remains the same: a genuine bond that nurtures and uplifts.

Family: The Bedrock of Love

Family represents the primal source of belonging. From infancy, our sense of self and security is intricately tied to our family's presence and care. The family dynamic is a complex interplay of roles, responsibilities, and emotions, but at its core, it offers:

- **Unconditional Love:** The purest form of acceptance, free from judgment.
- **Support System:** A safety net during life's trials and tribulations.
- **Shared Identity:** Traditions, values, and memories that create a sense of continuity.

For many, family serves as the anchor in the stormy seas of life. It is within the family unit that individuals often learn the language of love, the art of compromise, and the resilience required to navigate relationships.

However, family is not always defined by blood. In today's diverse societal structures, families can take myriad forms—from adoptive families to chosen families formed by close friends. What defines a family is not its composition but the depth of its connections and the love it fosters.

Community: The Collective Embrace

Beyond the intimate circles of friends and family lies the broader sense of community. Humans are inherently social beings, and communities offer a collective identity that transcends the individual. Communities are forged through shared interests, goals, or geographic proximity, and they provide:

- **A Sense of Belonging:** The comfort of being part of something larger than oneself.
- **Collective Purpose:** The motivation to contribute to a common good.
- **Support Networks:** Resources and connections that aid personal and collective growth.

From tribal societies to modern urban centers, communities have always played a pivotal role in human development. They act as a crucible for culture, innovation, and shared progress. Participation in community activities—be it through volunteering, religious congregations, or neighborhood events—can significantly enhance one's sense of belonging and fulfillment.

The Role of Belonging in Mental Health

Belonging and love are not luxuries but necessities for emotional and psychological health. The absence of these connections can lead to:

- **Loneliness:** A pervasive feeling of isolation that can harm mental health.
- **Anxiety and Depression:** Emotional distress stemming from a lack of connection or acceptance.
- **Low Self-Worth:** A diminished sense of value due to feelings of rejection or exclusion.

Conversely, strong bonds with friends, family, and community members provide resilience against life's adversities. They offer a buffer against stress and create a foundation for self-esteem and personal growth. The mere act of being understood and accepted can heal wounds that solitude cannot.

Challenges to Belonging in Modern Society

In an era of globalization and digital connectivity, paradoxically, feelings of isolation are on the rise. The fast-paced nature of modern life, coupled with the superficiality of some online interactions, can create barriers to genuine connection. Challenges include:

- **Social Fragmentation:** The erosion of traditional community structures.
- **Cultural Displacement:** The struggle to belong in a world of shifting identities.
- **Digital Disconnect:** The illusion of connection through social media that often lacks depth.

Addressing these challenges requires intentional efforts to cultivate and sustain meaningful relationships. It calls for a return to authentic interactions, where empathy and understanding are prioritized.

Cultivating Belonging and Love

To fulfill the need for belonging, one must actively engage in relationships and communities. This involves:

1. **Investing Time and Effort:** Building relationships requires consistency and care.
2. **Practicing Empathy:** Understanding and valuing others' perspectives strengthens bonds.
3. **Creating Safe Spaces:** Environments where individuals feel accepted and valued.
4. **Fostering Inclusivity:** Embracing diversity and ensuring no one feels excluded.

Belonging is a two-way street. While we seek connection, we must also offer it. Acts of kindness, active listening, and genuine interest in others' lives can create ripples of belonging that extend beyond individual relationships.

4.1.4: Self-Actualization – Creativity and Fulfillment

At the core of human existence lies the quest for meaning and the drive to fulfill our innate potential. This journey, often termed as self-actualization, is a deeply personal exploration of creativity, growth, and purpose. It is less about reaching a definitive end and more about engaging in a continuous process of becoming—a dynamic dance between our aspirations and the world we inhabit.

The Essence of Fulfillment

Fulfillment is not merely an accumulation of achievements or accolades; it is the alignment of one's actions with one's inner truth. It's a state where individuals move beyond societal expectations to embrace their authentic selves. This state is deeply intertwined with creativity, which acts as a bridge between the internal world of ideas and the external reality of expression.

Fulfillment stems from the realization that our unique contributions, however small, ripple outward to shape the collective human experience. It is the quiet joy of knowing that our existence carries meaning, both for ourselves and for others.

This state is deeply intertwined with creativity, which acts as a bridge between the internal world of ideas and the external reality of expression.

Fulfillment stems from the realization that our unique contributions, however small, ripple outward to shape the collective human experience. It is the quiet joy of knowing that our existence carries meaning, both for ourselves and for others.

Creativity as a Life Force

Creativity is not limited to the realms of art or invention; it is the essence of life itself. Every thought, every decision, every interaction holds the potential for creative expression. Creativity is the courage to see the world differently, to challenge norms, and to transform the ordinary into the extraordinary.

- **Exploration:** Creativity begins with curiosity—the willingness to ask questions and explore possibilities without fear of judgment.
- **Expression:** It flourishes when we give form to our ideas, whether through writing, problem-solving, or nurturing relationships.
- **Connection:** Creativity thrives in collaboration, where diverse perspectives converge to create something greater than the sum of its parts.

Engaging with creativity is not just about producing outcomes but also about experiencing the joy and vitality that come from living authentically.

Barriers to Creativity and Fulfillment

Despite its universality, the journey toward fulfillment is fraught with challenges. These barriers often arise from both external and internal forces:

- **Conformity:** The pressure to adhere to societal norms can stifle originality and self-expression.
- **Fear:** The fear of failure, rejection, or even success can inhibit our willingness to take creative risks.

- **Disconnection:** A lack of meaningful relationships or a sense of purpose can lead to stagnation.
- **Overwhelm:** The distractions of modern life—constant notifications, endless comparisons—can pull us away from our inner compass.

Overcoming these obstacles requires resilience, self-awareness, and the ability to reconnect with what truly matters.

Pathways to Fulfillment

Fulfillment is not a one-size-fits-all concept; it is as unique as the individual pursuing it. However, there are common pathways that can guide us toward this deeply rewarding state:

1. **Self-Discovery:** Take time to understand your passions, strengths, and values. Reflect on what brings you joy and what challenges ignite your curiosity.
2. **Mindful Living:** Engage fully with the present moment. Cultivate awareness of your thoughts, emotions, and surroundings to foster a deeper connection with life.
3. **Contribution:** Find ways to give back—whether through acts of kindness, sharing knowledge, or creating something meaningful. Contribution enriches both the giver and the receiver.
4. **Adaptability:** Embrace change and view setbacks as opportunities for growth. Flexibility allows us to navigate life's uncertainties with grace.

The Interplay of Fulfillment and Connection

True fulfillment often emerges in the context of relationships and community. While self-actualization is deeply personal, it is also inherently social. Our creative endeavors gain depth and resonance when shared with others. Through collaboration and mutual support, we weave a tapestry of experiences that elevate individual and collective well-being.

Whether mentoring a colleague, sharing a story, or simply listening with empathy, our connections provide a fertile ground for growth and fulfillment. They remind us that we are not isolated beings but integral parts of a larger whole.

A Dynamic Journey

Fulfillment is not static; it evolves as we grow and change. It is the continual process of aligning our inner aspirations with our external actions. This journey requires courage, curiosity, and an openness to transformation. Along the way, we learn that fulfillment is not found in perfection but in the act of striving, creating, and connecting.

4.2: The Reality of Fear

Fear, a shadow that follows us through the corridors of life, is both a primal instinct and a profound teacher. It is an undeniable force that shapes our decisions, our relationships, and our very understanding of existence. But to understand fear is to step closer to freedom—a freedom not from fear itself but from its dominion over us. By peeling back its layers, we uncover its origins, its illusions, and ultimately, its purpose in the grand narrative of our lives.

4.2.1: Fear of the Unknown

The unknown has always held a peculiar power over the human psyche. It is the vast, uncharted expanse of what lies beyond the edges of our comprehension. This fear, often unspoken, manifests in hesitation, anxiety, and a clinging to the familiar.

- **Why the Unknown Terrifies:** At its core, the fear of the unknown arises from our innate need for control. To step into the unknown is to relinquish the illusion of certainty, to admit that we cannot predict or dictate the outcomes of our actions. It is this vulnerability that makes the unknown so daunting.

- **The Paradox of the Unknown:** While we fear it, the unknown is also the source of all potential. Every discovery, every breakthrough, and every transformation begins in the territory of the unfamiliar. To resist it is to stagnate; to embrace it is to grow.
- **Navigating the Unknown:** The key to facing the unknown lies not in eliminating fear but in reframing it. Instead of viewing it as a threat, we can see it as an invitation—a call to adventure, to curiosity, and to the boundless possibilities that await beyond the horizon.

4.2.2: Fear vs. Perception and Overcoming Fear with Understanding

Fear and perception are inseparable companions. Fear often distorts our perception, painting exaggerated pictures of danger and failure. Yet, with understanding, we can recalibrate our vision, revealing the reality hidden behind the veil of fear.

- **The Illusions of Fear:** Fear thrives on half-truths and assumptions. It amplifies uncertainties, convincing us that worst-case scenarios are inevitable. In this way, fear becomes less about the actual threat and more about our interpretation of it.
- **Understanding Fear:** To overcome fear, we must first understand it. Fear is not an enemy but a signal. It alerts us to potential risks and compels us to prepare. When acknowledged without judgment, fear becomes a guide rather than a barrier.
- **The Power of Perspective:** Perspective is the antidote to fear's distortions. By stepping back and questioning the narratives fear constructs, we gain clarity. What is the evidence for this fear? What are the actual stakes? Such inquiries dismantle fear's grip, allowing us to respond with reason rather than reflex.
- **Action as Liberation:** The final step in overcoming fear is action. Fear feeds on inaction, growing stronger with every moment of hesitation. Conversely, even the smallest step forward diminishes its power. Through action, we transform fear from an obstacle into a catalyst for growth.

4.2.3: Mukti – Ultimate Liberation

At the heart of the human journey lies the quest for liberation—freedom not just from fear but from all forms of bondage. Mukti, a concept rooted in ancient philosophy, represents this ultimate liberation. It is the state of being unshackled, where the soul transcends the confines of ego, desire, and fear.

- **The Nature of Mukti:** Mukti is not merely the absence of fear; it is the presence of profound inner peace. It is the realization that our true essence is beyond the transient concerns of the material world. In Mukti, we experience unity with the infinite, a state where fear has no foothold.
- **The Path to Mukti:** Liberation begins with self-awareness. To achieve Mukti, one must first confront and understand the chains that bind them. These chains may take the form of attachments, beliefs, or unexamined fears. By shining the light of awareness on these shadows, we begin to dissolve them.
- **Fear as a Teacher:** Paradoxically, fear can be a guide on the path to Mukti. It points us to the areas where we are most attached, most resistant, and most in need of growth. By embracing fear rather than fleeing from it, we use it as a tool for liberation.
- **The Liberation of Letting Go:** At the heart of Mukti lies the act of surrender. To let go is not to give up but to release the illusion of control. It is to trust in the flow of life, to accept the impermanence of all things, and to find solace in the eternal present.

The Reality of Fear: A Closing Reflection

Fear, in all its forms, is an integral part of the human experience. It is not an adversary to be conquered but a companion to be understood. By facing the fear of the unknown, challenging fear's distortions, and walking the path toward Mukti, we transform fear from a source of suffering into a wellspring of wisdom.

In this transformation, we discover that fear is not a barrier but a doorway—one that leads us to deeper truths, greater freedom, and the ultimate realization of who we are. To embrace fear is to embrace life in all its uncertainty, complexity, and boundless potential.

CHAPTER 5: RESPECT, PASSION, AND COURAGE

The human spirit is a tapestry woven with threads of respect, passion, and courage. These three qualities are not mere virtues but dynamic forces that shape our relationships, our endeavors, and our journeys toward self-realization. In this chapter, we delve into the profound interplay between respect, passion, and courage, illuminating their roles as cornerstones of a meaningful life.

5.1: Respect and Passion

Respect and passion are not isolated ideals; they are intertwined energies that fuel the essence of human connection and purpose. While respect grounds us, offering stability and acknowledgment of value, passion ignites us, driving creativity and a zest for life. Together, they form a harmonious rhythm that empowers both the individual and the collective.

5.1.1: Respecting Yourself and Others

- **The Foundation of Respect:** Respect begins with acknowledgment—the recognition of inherent worth, both within ourselves and in others. It is not a transactional exchange but a universal truth that every being holds value simply by existing. To respect oneself is to honor one's potential, boundaries, and unique path. To respect others is to extend that same honor, creating spaces of mutual understanding and growth.
- **Self-Respect as the Core:** Self-respect is not about arrogance or self-importance; it is about aligning with your true self. It requires the courage to set boundaries, to stand firm in your values, and to prioritize your well-being without apology. When we respect ourselves, we cultivate an inner harmony that radiates outward, influencing how we engage with the world.
- **Respect in Relationships:** Respect is the bedrock of all meaningful relationships. It transcends agreement or similarity, allowing us to appreciate differences without judgment. Respecting others means listening with intention, valuing their perspectives, and treating them with dignity—even when conflict arises.

- **The Transformative Power of Respect:** Respect has the power to heal, to connect, and to elevate. It transforms interactions from superficial exchanges to profound connections, fostering trust and collaboration. In respecting ourselves and others, we lay the groundwork for a society rooted in empathy and equity.

5.1.2: Passion Through Respect

- **The Role of Respect in Passion:** Passion is often seen as a fiery, untamed force, but it is respect that channels this energy into purposeful action. When we respect our passions, we honor their importance in our lives. This respect drives us to nurture them, to invest time and effort, and to pursue them with unwavering commitment.
- **Respecting the Passion of Others:** Just as we honor our own passions, it is vital to respect the passions of others. Each individual's pursuits are reflections of their unique essence. By supporting and celebrating these passions, we create a culture of inspiration and collective growth.
- **Passion as a Catalyst for Respect:** Passion, when genuine, fosters respect. A person deeply engaged in their passion radiates authenticity, which commands admiration. This admiration is not rooted in envy but in a recognition of shared humanity—a reminder that we, too, can pursue what sets our souls alight.
- **The Synergy of Respect and Passion:** When respect and passion coexist, they create a synergy that fuels personal and communal evolution. Respect ensures that passion remains grounded, ethical, and inclusive, while passion infuses respect with vitality and direction.

5.1.3: The Relationship Between Time, Passion, and Respect

- **Time as a Reflection of Values:** Time is the most finite resource we possess, and how we spend it reveals our true priorities. Respecting time—both our own and that of others—is an act of reverence for life itself. It requires mindfulness, intention, and a commitment to living authentically.

- **Investing Time in Passion:** Passion demands time. It is through consistent dedication that passions are cultivated and transformed into mastery. To respect your passion is to allocate time for it, even amidst the demands of daily life. This investment is not a sacrifice but a fulfillment of your truest desires.
- **Respecting Others' Time:** Just as we value our own time, it is crucial to honor the time of others. Punctuality, attentiveness, and consideration are simple yet profound ways to demonstrate this respect. By valuing others' time, we strengthen relationships and build a foundation of trust.
- **The Interplay of Time, Passion, and Respect:** Time, passion, and respect are intricately connected. Respecting time allows passion to flourish; passion, in turn, imbues time with purpose and meaning. Together, they create a rhythm that aligns our actions with our deepest values.
- **Eternity in the Moment:** When we respect the present moment, we transcend the linear confines of time. Passion elevates this respect, transforming each moment into an opportunity for creativity and connection. In this space, we discover that the essence of life is not in its duration but in its depth.

The Harmony of Respect and Passion

Respect and passion are not opposing forces but complementary energies. Respect provides the structure and stability needed for passion to thrive, while passion infuses respect with vitality and purpose. Together, they empower us to live authentically, to connect deeply, and to contribute meaningfully to the world around us.

In understanding and embodying these principles, we step into a life of greater harmony and fulfillment. Respect and passion are not merely ideals to aspire to but practices to integrate into every moment. Through them, we honor the sacredness of existence and the boundless potential of the human spirit.

5.2: Mukti – The Convincing Story

Mukti, or liberation, is not a distant, esoteric goal but a profound reality that lies at the heart of existence. It is the ultimate alignment between the mental mind and the physical body, a state where harmony transcends the boundaries of duality. Mukti invites us to dissolve the illusions of separation, to understand our essence, and to experience the world with clarity and authenticity.

5.2.1: Aligning the Mental Mind and Physical Body

The journey to Mukti begins with the alignment of the mental mind and the physical body. This alignment is not merely a balance but a unification of two dimensions of our being. The mental mind, governed by thoughts and perceptions, often drifts away from the reality of the physical body, which is rooted in the tangible, present moment. To achieve Mukti, these two realms must work in harmony.

- **Bridging the Gap:** Alignment starts with awareness. By observing the dissonance between our thoughts and actions, we can begin to bridge the gap. Mindfulness practices, such as meditation and conscious breathing, serve as tools to synchronize the mind and body.
- **Flow and Presence:** When the mental mind and physical body are aligned, we enter a state of flow. In this state, every action becomes effortless, every thought purposeful. Presence replaces distraction, allowing us to engage fully with life.
- **Integration, Not Domination:** Mukti does not demand the domination of one aspect over the other. Instead, it calls for integration—a recognition that the mental and physical are two facets of the same whole, each essential and interdependent.

5.2.2: Mental Mind - The Five Senses

The five senses are not just channels through which we experience the world—they are the bridges between our mental mind and the physical reality around us. These senses shape our perceptions, guide our thoughts, and color our experiences. By understanding their role, we can bring our mental mind into harmony with the body.

Sight

Sight is often regarded as the most powerful of the senses. It is through our eyes that we first engage with the world, and it is through vision that we form our judgments and emotions. However, true alignment with the mental mind calls for more than simply seeing what is before us. It is about seeing beyond the surface, perceiving the deeper essence of things. By training ourselves to look with awareness, we begin to see not just the world, but also the truth within it.

Hearing

Hearing connects us to the rhythm of life itself. The sounds of nature, the voices of others, and even the quiet hum of the world around us all influence our mental state. When we cultivate deep listening, we create space for clarity and understanding. True listening goes beyond the noise—it aligns our mind with the silent currents that flow beneath the surface, fostering inner peace and insight.

Taste

Taste is often linked to indulgence, but it holds the potential to be a path to mindfulness. Every flavor we experience—whether sweet, bitter, or sour—reflects the richness and diversity of life. By savoring each taste fully, we bring our attention to the present moment, grounding the mental mind in the now. Each bite is an invitation to engage with the world more deeply and consciously.

Touch

Touch is the sense that connects us to the physical world and to each other. It is through touch that we experience intimacy, comfort, and presence.

Whether the warmth of a loved one's hand or the feel of the earth beneath our feet, touch grounds us in the reality of our bodies. Conscious touch, when practiced with intention, nurtures the alignment of the mind and body, fostering a deeper connection to the world around us.

Smell

Smell is the most primal of the senses, capable of evoking memories and emotions with a potency unmatched by the other senses. A single scent can transport us to another time or place, stirring feelings and insights from the depths of the subconscious. By becoming more aware of our sense of smell, we reconnect with the present moment and unlock deeper layers of our mental mind, tapping into memories and emotions that guide us on our journey of self-awareness.

In exploring these senses, we not only enhance our understanding of the world but also deepen our connection to the mind and body. Each sense is a gateway to a more profound experience of life, one that allows us to align our mental mind with the physical world in a harmonious dance of perception and presence.

5.2.3: Physical Body – Components

The physical body, our tangible presence in the world, is a complex system of interdependent components. Each part plays a vital role in maintaining our existence and serves as a gateway to understanding the essence of Mukti.

Skin

The skin is the boundary between the self and the external world. It is both a shield and a bridge, protecting us while enabling connection. Respecting the skin as a living, breathing organ fosters awareness of our physicality.

Flesh

Flesh represents the strength and vulnerability of the human form. It embodies the duality of existence, reminding us of our mortality and resilience. Honoring the flesh is a step toward embracing our physical reality.

Organs

The organs are the silent workers of the body, sustaining life through their ceaseless functions. By nurturing their health, we cultivate gratitude for the unseen efforts that keep us alive.

Skeleton

The skeleton, the framework of our body, symbolizes stability and structure. It supports our movements and protects our core. Recognizing its importance grounds us in the reality of our physical form.

Blood

Blood, the life force that flows through us, connects every part of the body. It is a reminder of our interconnectedness, both within and beyond ourselves. By honoring this vital essence, we align with the rhythm of life.

Mukti as Wholeness

Mukti is the realization that the mental mind and physical body are not separate entities but expressions of a unified whole. By aligning these dimensions through the understanding of our senses and components, we transcend fragmentation and experience the oneness of existence. This journey is not about escaping reality but embracing it fully, with clarity, passion, and respect.

5.3: Validating Your Feelings

In the boundless journey of life, emotions are not merely fleeting moments or transient responses to external stimuli. They are the undercurrent that shapes our very essence, the whispers of our soul that speak truths we often fail to hear in the clamor of the world. Emotions are neither good nor bad; they simply are. They exist as an integral part of our humanity, woven into the tapestry of our being, and to deny them is to deny the very essence of who we are.

To validate your feelings is to accept that these emotions—whether joy, sorrow, anger, or peace—hold inherent value. They are not accidental nor are they insignificant. In fact, each emotion is a messenger, a bearer of wisdom from within. It is easy to dismiss our feelings as inconvenient or illogical, particularly in a world that often prizes rationality and control over emotional expression. But the truth is that emotions are neither illogical nor irrational. They are a reflection of our experiences, our values, our fears, and our desires. They are, in essence, our internal compass, guiding us through the chaos of life. To validate your feelings is to acknowledge this truth and honor your emotional self without shame or apology.

The validation of one's emotions does not mean to indulge in them blindly or to let them dictate your actions. It does not imply surrendering to every whim or mood that arises. Rather, it means recognizing that your feelings are valid expressions of your internal reality. You may not always understand why you feel the way you do, and that is okay. But to deny or repress these feelings only leads to further inner turmoil. When we invalidate our emotions, we create a disconnect between our inner world and the world around us. This dissonance breeds confusion, self-doubt, and a sense of alienation. However, when we validate our feelings, we allow ourselves to come into alignment with our truth. We give ourselves permission to exist fully, to experience life in all its complexities, and to grow from the rich soil of our emotional landscape.

5.3.1: Expressing Your Feelings

The expression of feelings is the art of translating the language of the heart into the words and actions of the world. It is one thing to feel deeply, but it is quite another to communicate those feelings effectively. In a world that often encourages silence, conformity, and emotional restraint, the act of expressing your feelings is both revolutionary and necessary. To express your emotions is to give voice to your truth, to make visible what is often hidden beneath the surface of our everyday interactions.

Expression is not limited to words. While verbal communication is one way to share your feelings, it is far from the only one. Art, music, movement, and even silence are all powerful forms of emotional expression. The medium through which you express yourself may vary, but the essence remains the same: it is the act of externalizing the internal, of making tangible what is intangible. Through expression, we not only communicate with others, but we also communicate with ourselves. It is a form of self-discovery, a means of understanding the deeper currents of our soul. When we express our feelings, we release them from the confines of our minds and bodies, allowing them to flow freely into the world. In doing so, we not only honor ourselves but also invite others to do the same.

Yet, despite the power and beauty of emotional expression, many of us struggle with it. We fear judgment, rejection, or misunderstanding. We are taught, often from an early age, that some emotions are more acceptable than others. Anger is frowned upon; vulnerability is seen as weakness; joy is dismissed as excessive. We learn to suppress our feelings in the name of propriety, civili ty, or self-control. But in doing so, we stifle our authentic selves. We silence the very essence of who we are, and in turn, we deprive the world of the unique light that only we can offer.

Expressing your feelings is not about seeking approval or validation from others. It is about honoring your own emotional truth and allowing it to be seen and heard. It is about creating space for your feelings to exist in their full complexity, without fear of judgment or rejection. When you express your emotions honestly and authentically, you invite others to do the same. You create a space where vulnerability is not only accepted but celebrated. In this space, connections are formed not on the surface level, but in the deep, unspoken understanding that we are all, at our core, emotional beings.

And it is through this shared humanity that true intimacy and understanding are born.

5.3.2: Processing Pain and Betrayal

Pain and betrayal are perhaps the most profound and challenging experiences we face in life. They shake us to our core, unraveling the fabric of our trust and security. Yet, despite their intensity, pain and betrayal are also powerful teachers. They strip away the illusions we cling to, forcing us to confront the truth of who we are and what we value. In their wake, we often feel lost, confused, and broken. But if we are willing to sit with our pain, to lean into it rather than running from it, we may find that it is in these moments of suffering that we learn the most about ourselves.

To process pain is to allow it to move through you. It is not about avoiding or suppressing the hurt, but rather about feeling it in its entirety. Pain, like all emotions, is temporary. It may seem endless in the moment, but if we allow ourselves to experience it fully, it will eventually pass. The key is not to resist it but to surrender to it. To sit with the discomfort and allow it to reveal its wisdom. Pain teaches us about our boundaries, our needs, and our capacity for resilience. It shows us what truly matters to us and forces us to reevaluate our priorities. In this way, pain becomes a catalyst for transformation. It is through the crucible of suffering that we are forged into stronger, wiser versions of ourselves.

Betrayal, in particular, is a form of pain that cuts deeply. It is not just the loss of trust in another person, but the shattering of our own beliefs and expectations. Betrayal forces us to confront the fragility of our relationships and the fallibility of those we place our trust in. It leaves us questioning not only the other person but also ourselves. How could we have been so blind? What did we miss? What did we do wrong? These questions can torment us, but they are also the very questions that lead to growth. Betrayal is an opportunity to examine our own vulnerabilities and to learn from the experience.

It is a chance to rebuild our trust, not only in others but in ourselves.

To process betrayal, we must first allow ourselves to grieve. Grief is the natural response to loss, and betrayal is, without a doubt, a form of loss. We lose our sense of safety, our belief in the other person, and perhaps even our faith in the world. But grief is not a sign of weakness; it is a testament to our capacity to love and trust in the first place. It is only through grieving that we can begin to heal. Once we allow ourselves to fully feel the pain of betrayal, we can begin the process of forgiveness. Forgiveness does not mean excusing the actions of others, but it does mean releasing ourselves from the grip of anger and resentment. It is about freeing ourselves from the chains of the past and choosing to move forward with a renewed sense of strength and clarity.

In processing pain and betrayal, we must remember that these experiences are not the end of our story. They are chapters in a much larger narrative, one that is still unfolding. And while we may not have control over the events that cause us pain, we do have control over how we respond. We can choose to let pain define us, or we can choose to let it refine us. The choice is ours.

5.3.3: Embracing Emotions Without Shame

In a world that often teaches us to suppress our emotions, to hide our vulnerability, and to present a polished, perfect version of ourselves, embracing emotions without shame is an act of radical self-acceptance. Emotions, in all their complexity, are a natural and essential part of being human. Yet, for many of us, there is a pervasive sense of shame that surrounds the expression of certain emotions. We feel ashamed of our sadness, as though it is a weakness. We feel ashamed of our anger, as though it is something to be hidden or controlled. We feel ashamed of our joy, as though it is too much, too loud, too visible. But the truth is that emotions are not something to be ashamed of. They are a part of who we are, and they deserve to be acknowledged, expressed, and honored.

To embrace your emotions without shame is to free yourself from the societal constraints that tell you what is acceptable and what is not. It is to let go of the belief that you must always be in control, always composed, always "together." It is to allow yourself to feel deeply, to laugh loudly, to cry when necessary, and to express anger in a healthy way. Embracing your emotions is not about indulgence or excess. It is about being true to yourself, about honoring your feelings as they arise, without judgment or self-recrimination.

In this process, we must also learn to accept the emotions of others. Just as we are entitled to our own emotional experiences, so too are others. To embrace emotions without shame is to create a space of compassion, understanding, and connection. It is to acknowledge that we are all human, that we all experience pain, joy, anger, and fear, and that none of these emotions make us any less worthy of love, respect, or acceptance.

In the end, emotions are not obstacles to be overcome, but the very fabric of our existence. They are the colors on the canvas of our lives, the music in the soundtrack of our journey. To embrace them without shame is to live fully, authentically, and without reservation. It is to be unapologetically human. And it is in this unapologetic embrace of our emotional selves that we find our true freedom.

5.4: Principles of Faith and Trust

Faith and trust are the twin pillars that support our journey through life. They are the invisible forces that guide our decisions, shape our relationships, and anchor us in times of uncertainty. These principles—faith, trust, confidence, and hope—are not merely abstract ideals; they are the very foundation of our emotional and spiritual resilience. In the face of life's unpredictability, they offer us stability and direction, even when the path ahead is unclear. To understand and cultivate these principles is to learn how to navigate life with grace, courage, and an unwavering sense of purpose.

5.4.1: Faith – The Umbrella in the Rain

Faith is often likened to an umbrella in a storm. It is the protective shield that shields us from life's tempests, the steadfast companion that keeps us grounded when everything else seems to be falling apart. Faith is not blind belief or naïve optimism; it is the deep-rooted conviction that there is meaning, purpose, and guidance even in the most challenging of circumstances. It is the trust that, despite the storms of life, we will emerge stronger, wiser, and more resilient.

Faith is an act of surrender. It is not about controlling every outcome or demanding certainty in every situation. Instead, it is the willingness to embrace uncertainty and believe that there is something greater at work. Faith is not a passive waiting for things to improve; it is an active participation in the unfolding of our lives. It is the belief that, even when we cannot see the way forward, there is a force, whether divine, universal, or internal, that is guiding us toward the right destination.

Faith is the quiet strength that sustains us through adversity. It is the light in the darkness that gives us the courage to take the next step, even when we cannot see what lies ahead. It is the confidence that, despite the rain, we are not alone, and that there is a purpose to the struggle. Just as an umbrella shields us from the downpour, faith shields us from despair, offering us protection and comfort when life feels overwhelming. In moments of doubt, faith reminds us that the storm is temporary, and that the sun will shine again.

5.4.2: Trust – The Laughing Baby

Trust is the essence of connection. It is the invisible thread that binds us to others, creating the foundation for meaningful relationships and shared experiences. Trust is often likened to the innocent, unguarded nature of a laughing baby. When a baby laughs, there is no hesitation, no suspicion, no fear. There is a complete surrender to the moment, an open-hearted belief that the world is safe, kind, and full of joy. This is the purity of trust—an innate understanding that we are supported, loved, and cared for, even in the face of uncertainty.

Trust is built over time, through consistent actions and mutual understanding. It is not something that can be demanded or forced; it must be earned. Trust is fragile, like a delicate flower, requiring nurture, patience, and attention. It is a gift that, once given, can transform relationships, creating a bond that is both deep and enduring. Trust allows us to be vulnerable, to open our hearts to others, and to believe in their intentions. It is the foundation of empathy, compassion, and shared growth.

Yet trust is not without its challenges. Betrayal, disappointment, and betrayal can erode trust, leaving us hesitant to open ourselves to others. But even in these moments of pain, trust is not lost forever. It is a renewable resource, one that can be rebuilt with time, effort, and understanding. Just as a baby learns to trust the world through repeated experiences of care and love, we too can rebuild our trust in others through consistent, honest, and loving actions.

Trust is not simply about relying on others; it is also about trusting ourselves. It is the belief that we have the wisdom, strength, and resilience to navigate life's challenges. When we trust ourselves, we create the foundation for healthy, fulfilling relationships with others. Trust is the recognition that we are worthy of love, support, and respect, and that we have the ability to offer the same in return. It is the laughter of the baby—pure, unguarded, and full of joy—that reminds us of the beauty and power of trust.

5.4.3: Confidence – Setting the Alarm Without Assurance

Confidence is the quiet certainty that we are capable of facing whatever challenges life presents. It is the internal knowing that we have the strength, skill, and resilience to navigate the unknown. Confidence is often likened to setting an alarm without assurance. We do not know for certain that the alarm will go off, but we trust that it will. In the same way, confidence is not about having absolute certainty or assurance in every situation. It is about trusting that, regardless of the outcome, we are equipped to handle whatever comes our way.

Confidence is born from experience. It is the cumulative result of facing challenges, learning from mistakes, and persevering through difficult circumstances. Each experience, whether successful or not, adds to our reservoir of confidence. It is the recognition that we have faced adversity before and emerged stronger, and that we will continue to do so in the future. Confidence is not arrogance; it is the quiet, unshakable belief that we are capable, even when the outcome is uncertain.

Setting the alarm without assurance is an act of faith in our own abilities. It is the belief that, even if things do not go as planned, we have the resilience to adapt, learn, and grow. Confidence is not about avoiding failure; it is about embracing it as a natural part of the process. When we set the alarm without assurance, we are trusting that, even if the alarm doesn't go off as expected, we have the wisdom and strength to handle the situation. Confidence is not the absence of fear or doubt; it is the ability to move forward despite them.

Confidence is also about self-compassion. It is the understanding that we are not perfect, that we will make mistakes, and that failure is not a reflection of our worth. Confidence is the ability to learn from failure, to grow from setbacks, and to continue moving forward with courage and determination. It is the willingness to set the alarm without knowing whether it will go off, and to trust that, regardless of the outcome, we will be okay.

5.4.4: Hope – Planning for Tomorrow

Hope is the quiet force that drives us forward, even in the darkest of times. It is the belief that, despite the challenges we face, there is always the possibility of a better tomorrow. Hope is not blind optimism; it is the belief that change is possible, that growth is always within reach, and that the future holds promise, even when the present feels uncertain. Hope is the act of planning for tomorrow, even when we cannot predict what it will bring.

Hope is the fuel that keeps us moving, even when the road ahead is unclear. It is the belief that our efforts, no matter how small, will eventually lead to positive change. Hope is not about waiting for things to get better on their own; it is about taking action, even when the outcome is uncertain. It is the recognition that, while we cannot control everything, we can control how we respond to the challenges we face.

Planning for tomorrow is an act of hope. It is the belief that our actions today will shape the future we desire. Hope is not about wishing for a better tomorrow; it is about taking steps, however small, to create that future. Hope is the recognition that, no matter how difficult the present moment may be, the future holds the potential for growth, transformation, and renewal.

In times of uncertainty, hope reminds us that there is always the possibility of a better tomorrow. It is the belief that, even in the darkest moments, there is light on the horizon. Hope is the vision of a future where our dreams are realized, where our efforts bear fruit, and where we find peace, joy, and fulfillment. Hope is the anchor that keeps us grounded, the light that guides us forward, and the fuel that drives us to keep moving, no matter what challenges we face.

5.5: Cooperation and Love

Cooperation and love are two of the most powerful forces that bind us together as human beings. They shape the way we interact with others, create lasting relationships, and influence the world around us. When we cooperate, we come together to achieve common goals, setting aside our individual interests for the greater good. When we love, we open our hearts to others, embracing their flaws and celebrating their virtues. These two forces—cooperation and love—are deeply interconnected, each nurturing and enhancing the other. Together, they create the foundation for meaningful connections, collaborative success, and emotional fulfillment. In this exploration of cooperation and love, we will delve into their elements and expressions, uncovering how they shape our interactions and enrich our lives.

5.5.1: Elements of Cooperation

Cooperation is the art of working together to achieve shared objectives, overcoming individual differences and obstacles to create something greater than the sum of its parts. It is the ability to come together with others, aligning your actions and intentions toward a common goal. While cooperation can manifest in many forms, certain key elements serve as the foundation for successful collaboration.

Asking Without Expecting

At the heart of cooperation is the principle of asking without expecting. This means approaching others with humility, openness, and respect, without assuming that they owe you anything in return. In cooperative relationships, we ask for help or support, but we do so without demanding or imposing conditions. Asking without expecting is rooted in the belief that people are not obligated to give, but that the act of asking creates a space for generosity, understanding, and mutual benefit.

When we ask without expecting, we remove the burden of entitlement and open the door to authentic collaboration. We give others the freedom to choose how they wish to respond, creating an environment of trust and respect. This approach fosters a sense of shared responsibility and empowers everyone involved to contribute their unique talents, perspectives, and resources to the collective effort.

In the context of cooperation, asking without expecting also involves recognizing that we may not always receive what we want, but that the process of asking itself is valuable. It is an invitation for dialogue, a call for understanding, and an opportunity to learn from others. When we ask without expecting, we embrace the beauty of the collaborative process, understanding that the outcome is shaped by the collective contributions of all involved.

Accepting Change and Compromising

Cooperation is inherently dynamic, requiring us to adapt, evolve, and compromise as we work together. Accepting change and compromising are essential elements of successful cooperation because they allow us to navigate differences and find common ground. In any collaborative effort, there will inevitably be differences in opinion, priorities, and perspectives. The ability to accept these differences, rather than resist or ignore them, is what enables cooperation to thrive.

Accepting change means being open to new ideas, new ways of doing things, and the possibility of unexpected outcomes. It requires a willingness to let go of rigid expectations and embrace the fluidity of the process. In cooperative efforts, change is often the result of collective input, creative solutions, and evolving circumstances. Rather than viewing change as a threat or disruption, we learn to see it as an opportunity for growth, improvement, and innovation. Compromise is equally important in cooperation. It involves finding a middle ground where all parties feel heard, respected, and valued. Compromise does not mean sacrificing one's core values or settling for less than what is fair; rather, it is about finding solutions that work for everyone involved. In the spirit of cooperation, compromise is a way to balance individual needs with the collective goal, ensuring that no one feels left out or unheard.

When we accept change and embrace compromise, we create an environment where cooperation can flourish. We learn to adapt, to negotiate, and to collaborate in ways that honor both individual and collective needs. This flexibility and willingness to meet others halfway are what make cooperation possible, even in the face of challenges and disagreements.

Win-Win Solutions

A core principle of cooperation is the pursuit of win-win solutions. A win-win solution is one in which all parties benefit, creating a sense of mutual satisfaction and shared success. It is the opposite of a zero-sum mentality, where one person's gain is seen as another person's loss. In cooperative relationships, the goal is to find outcomes that are mutually beneficial, where everyone involved feels that their needs, desires, and contributions are acknowledged and valued.

Achieving win-win solutions requires creativity, open-mindedness, and a willingness to explore different possibilities. It involves seeking solutions that are fair, equitable, and inclusive, and that respect the interests of all parties. Win-win solutions are not always easy to come by, but they are the hallmark of successful cooperation, as they foster long-term collaboration, trust, and respect.

In practice, win-win solutions often require negotiation, compromise, and the ability to think beyond one's immediate interests. They are about creating value for everyone involved, ensuring that no one is left behind. When we work toward win-win solutions, we shift the focus from individual gain to collective well-being, creating a sense of shared purpose and achievement.

5.5.2: Expressions of Love

Love is the emotional and spiritual force that binds us to one another. It is the capacity to care for others, to feel empathy and compassion, and to nurture meaningful connections. Love is expressed in countless ways, from the quiet acts of kindness to the deep, unspoken bonds that unite us. In the context of cooperation, love is the emotional glue that holds everything together, enabling us to work together with empathy, understanding, and mutual respect. There are several key expressions of love that enhance cooperation and strengthen relationships.

Listening

Listening is one of the most powerful expressions of love. It is the act of giving our full attention to another person, allowing them to be heard, understood, and validated. When we listen, we create a space for others to express themselves without judgment or interruption. Listening is an act of love because it shows that we value the other person's thoughts, feelings, and experiences.

In cooperative relationships, listening is essential for building trust, resolving conflicts, and fostering mutual understanding. It allows us to gain insight into others' perspectives, needs, and desires, which in turn helps us to work together more effectively. Listening is not just about hearing words; it is about being present, engaging with empathy, and acknowledging the emotions and intentions behind the words.

When we listen with love, we communicate that we care about the other person's well-being, and that their voice matters. Listening is a form of respect, a way of honoring the humanity of others. In the context of cooperation, listening helps to create a foundation of mutual respect and understanding, allowing for more productive and harmonious collaboration.

Speaking

Speaking is another powerful expression of love. It is the way we communicate our thoughts, feelings, and needs to others. When we speak with love, we choose our words carefully, with kindness, respect, and clarity. Speaking with love means communicating honestly, but also with sensitivity and compassion. It is about sharing our truth while being mindful of how our words impact others.

In cooperative relationships, speaking with love fosters open, honest communication, which is essential for resolving misunderstandings, setting expectations, and building trust. When we speak with love, we create a safe space for others to express themselves as well, leading to more meaningful and productive conversations. Speaking with love also involves expressing appreciation, offering encouragement, and affirming others' contributions.

Forgiving

Forgiveness is an expression of love that frees us from the burdens of resentment, anger, and hurt. It is the act of letting go of past wrongs, releasing the grip of negative emotions, and choosing to move forward with compassion. Forgiveness does not mean condoning harmful behavior or forgetting the past; rather, it is about releasing the emotional weight of past hurts in order to create space for healing, growth, and renewal.

In cooperative relationships, forgiveness is essential for maintaining harmony and trust. When we forgive, we allow ourselves and others to move past mistakes and miscommunications, creating an environment where cooperation can thrive. Forgiveness enables us to learn from our experiences, rather than being held hostage by them, and to approach future interactions with a spirit of understanding and openness.

Trusting

Trust is the ultimate expression of love. It is the willingness to be vulnerable, to rely on others, and to believe in their intentions and capabilities. Trust is an act of love because it shows that we have faith in the other person's integrity, wisdom, and care. In cooperative relationships, trust is the bedrock on which everything else is built. Without trust, cooperation becomes impossible.

Trusting others requires courage and vulnerability. It means letting go of control, accepting uncertainty, and believing that others will act in our best interests. When we trust with love, we give others the freedom to be themselves, to make mistakes, and to grow. Trusting is a gift that fosters connection, deepens relationships, and strengthens the cooperative bond.

5.6: Courage – The Six Dimensions

Courage is often romanticized as the bold, dramatic acts of bravery we see in heroes or legends. However, in its essence, courage is far more subtle, complex, and multidimensional. It is the willingness to act in the face of fear, uncertainty, or difficulty, and it manifests in various forms depending on the challenges we face. True courage does not just emerge in extraordinary circumstances but is an intrinsic quality that can be cultivated across different aspects of our lives. The six dimensions of courage—moral, spiritual, physical, social, intellectual, and emotional—each serve as a unique lens through which we can explore the multifaceted nature of human bravery. In this section, we will examine each dimension, uncovering its significance and understanding how it contributes to the broader tapestry of courage.

5.6.1: Moral Courage – Ethics and Integrity

Moral courage is the ability to stand up for what is right, even when it is difficult, unpopular, or fraught with personal risk. It is the strength to make ethical decisions in the face of opposition, fear, or temptation. Unlike physical courage, which is often linked to physical acts of bravery, moral courage pertains to our inner compass—our integrity, our principles, and our commitment to doing what is just, even when no one is watching.

In a world where shortcuts, compromises, and ethical lapses are common, moral courage is a rare and invaluable trait. It is the courage to speak out against injustice, to challenge systems of corruption, or to act according to one's beliefs, even when faced with significant personal cost. It often requires us to confront uncomfortable truths about ourselves, our society, and our world.

Moral courage manifests in everyday decisions—whether it's calling out unethical behavior in the workplace, standing up for a friend who is being mistreated, or refusing to participate in harmful practices. It requires the ability to face criticism, rejection, or even punishment for the sake of maintaining one's ethical standards.

Ultimately, moral courage is about living with integrity. It is not just about making the right choice when the consequences are clear but having the strength to act in alignment with one's values even when the outcome is uncertain. This form of courage allows us to maintain our humanity and dignity, ensuring that we remain true to our highest ideals.

5.6.2: Spiritual Courage – Grappling with Faith and Purpose

Spiritual courage is the fortitude to confront the mysteries of existence, the uncertainties of faith, and the profound questions of life and death. It is the courage to explore the depths of our spiritual beliefs and values, even when the answers seem elusive or when doubt clouds our understanding. Spiritual courage does not necessarily relate to religion; rather, it is the bravery to seek meaning and purpose in life, to connect with a higher power or principle, and to live in accordance with our spiritual truths.

This form of courage often emerges during moments of existential crisis—when we question the meaning of life, struggle with loss, or experience a deep sense of disconnection. It is the strength to continue searching for purpose, even when faced with overwhelming uncertainty or a sense of spiritual dryness. It requires the resilience to embrace faith without needing all the answers and to trust in a larger narrative that extends beyond our individual lives.

Spiritual courage can also be seen in the pursuit of personal transformation. It is the courage to confront our inner darkness, to question old beliefs, and to embrace new perspectives. Whether it is embarking on a spiritual journey, seeking reconciliation with a higher power, or embracing a philosophy that promotes inner peace, spiritual courage allows us to navigate the uncertainties of life with a sense of purpose and faith.

At its core, spiritual courage is about embracing the unknown with humility and trust, allowing us to find deeper meaning in life, even amidst its challenges and mysteries. It empowers us to confront the paradoxes of existence and to live authentically according to our spiritual convictions.

5.6.3: Physical Courage – Bravery Against Bodily Risks

Physical courage is the bravery to face bodily harm or danger without succumbing to fear. It is the willingness to put oneself at risk to protect others, to pursue a cause, or to achieve a goal, even when it involves physical danger. This is the type of courage that is often most easily recognized because it is displayed in dramatic, high-stakes situations—such as a soldier going into battle, a firefighter rescuing someone from a burning building, or a parent shielding their child from harm.

However, physical courage is not limited to grand gestures. It can also be found in the everyday actions that require us to push past our physical discomforts. Whether it's challenging ourselves to take on a physically demanding task, facing an illness or injury with resilience, or overcoming personal physical limitations, physical courage involves confronting fear and pushing through the barriers of our own body.

Physical courage also requires mental fortitude. It is not simply the absence of fear but the ability to act despite it. The physical challenges we face often mirror the emotional and psychological struggles we experience. The courage to push beyond pain, exhaustion, or injury is a reflection of our deeper determination and willpower.

Physical courage, in essence, is about acknowledging the fragility of our bodies and yet choosing to move forward, regardless of the risks. It teaches us to honor our physical limits while also expanding them through acts of bravery and resilience.

5.6.4: Social Courage – Leadership Amid Rejection

Social courage is the bravery to stand alone when the crowd is against you. It is the courage to take risks in relationships, to speak out for what is right, and to lead with authenticity, even when faced with social rejection or isolation. In a world where conformity often reigns, social courage is the ability to stay true to one's beliefs, values, and identity, even when they are not popular or accepted by the majority.

Social courage is especially important in leadership roles. It is the courage to lead with conviction, to challenge the status quo, and to take responsibility for difficult decisions. A leader with social courage does not shy away from making unpopular choices if they believe it is in the best interest of their team or cause. They understand that leadership often requires standing up to pressure, overcoming resistance, and navigating the complexities of human dynamics.

Moreover, social courage is essential for those who seek to create positive change in society. Whether advocating for social justice, supporting marginalized communities, or speaking out against harmful practices, social courage is the driving force behind movements that challenge societal norms. It requires the resilience to face rejection, criticism, and even hostility while staying committed to the cause.

In personal relationships, social courage allows us to be vulnerable, to express our true selves, and to risk emotional intimacy, knowing that it may not always be reciprocated. It is the courage to be authentic in a world that often values superficiality and appearances over genuine connection.

5.6.5: Intellectual Courage – Engaging with Challenging Ideas

Intellectual courage is the willingness to confront ideas, beliefs, and perspectives that challenge our own, even when they provoke discomfort or force us to reconsider long-held convictions. It is the courage to engage with difficult ideas, to explore the unknown, and to question established norms in the pursuit of knowledge and truth.

In an age of information overload, intellectual courage is more important than ever. It involves the ability to think critically, to engage with complex issues, and to consider perspectives that may be uncomfortable or unsettling. Intellectual courage is not about being obstinate or dogmatic; rather, it is about being open to growth and transformation through the power of ideas.

This form of courage is particularly important in the realm of education, research, and innovation. It is the courage to ask the hard questions, to challenge assumptions, and to explore new avenues of thought, even when it feels easier to stay within the boundaries of conventional wisdom. Intellectual courage enables us to break through intellectual stagnation and expand the horizons of human understanding.

Moreover, intellectual courage is essential for personal growth. It allows us to confront our own biases, to reassess our beliefs, and to evolve in our thinking. By engaging with challenging ideas, we develop the flexibility to see the world from multiple perspectives, which ultimately enriches our understanding and deepens our wisdom.

5.6.6: Emotional Courage – Embracing the Full Spectrum of Emotions

Emotional courage is the bravery to experience, express, and process the full range of human emotions. It is the courage to face pain, grief, joy, love, and fear without denial or suppression. Emotional courage is the strength to feel deeply, to acknowledge the vulnerability of being human, and to engage with emotions in a healthy, constructive way.

In many cultures, emotions are often seen as weaknesses to be hidden or controlled. However, emotional courage challenges this view by recognizing that emotions are integral to the human experience. Emotions are not something to be feared or avoided; they are the language of the heart, signaling our deepest desires, fears, and truths.

Emotional courage allows us to embrace vulnerability, to express our feelings authentically, and to heal from emotional wounds. It is the courage to cry when we are sad, to speak up when we are hurt, and to open our hearts when we are afraid of being rejected. It also means the courage to feel joy, to celebrate our successes, and to express love without fear of being judged or hurt.

By cultivating emotional courage, we learn to accept ourselves fully, including our imperfections and vulnerabilities. We become more resilient, able to navigate life's emotional ups and downs with grace and self-compassion. Emotional courage enables us to form deeper, more meaningful connections with others, as we allow ourselves to be seen in our full humanity.

5.7: Elements of Courage

Courage is often viewed as a singular, heroic trait that appears in the face of danger or adversity. However, courage is not a monolith; it is a rich, multifaceted virtue that encompasses various elements, each contributing to the overall strength we need to navigate life's challenges. At its core, courage is the ability to confront fear, uncertainty, or pain with determination and resolve. Yet, the true depth of courage is revealed in the subtle and often unseen components that form its foundation. These elements—self-confidence and conviction, integrity and compassion, leadership and strength in adversity, and embracing the unknown and taking action—are the building blocks of courageous living.

In this section, we will explore these elements in depth, understanding how they contribute to the broader tapestry of courage and why each one is essential in the pursuit of a life lived boldly, authentically, and with purpose.

5.7.1: Self-Confidence and Conviction

Self-confidence is the quiet, steadfast belief in one's abilities, decisions, and worth. It is the foundation upon which all acts of courage are built. Without self-confidence, we are paralyzed by doubt and fear, unable to take the risks or make the choices necessary to pursue our goals. Confidence is not about arrogance or overestimation of one's abilities; rather, it is a deep, unshakable trust in oneself that allows us to face challenges with the belief that we are capable of overcoming them.

Self-confidence does not emerge overnight. It is cultivated through consistent action, self-reflection, and learning from both successes and failures. When we believe in ourselves, we become less afraid of failure, because we understand that setbacks are part of the journey. Confidence allows us to step forward into the unknown with the conviction that we have the inner resources to adapt and succeed, regardless of the obstacles in our path.

Conviction is the unwavering commitment to our beliefs, values, and goals. It is the strength of purpose that drives us to act in alignment with what we hold to be true, even when the road is difficult. Conviction often manifests as a deep sense of moral clarity—a belief in a cause, a principle, or a vision that transcends the fleeting doubts or external pressures we may encounter.

When combined, self-confidence and conviction form a powerful synergy. Confidence gives us the strength to pursue our goals, while conviction keeps us focused on the greater purpose. Together, they provide the internal fuel to push through the toughest challenges and stay true to our course, no matter how daunting the journey may seem.

5.7.2: Integrity and Compassion

Integrity is the adherence to moral and ethical principles, even when it is inconvenient, difficult, or unpopular. It is the foundation of trust and authenticity. A person of integrity acts in accordance with their values, regardless of external pressures or the potential for personal gain. Integrity is not something that can be turned on or off—it is a consistent, guiding force that shapes every decision and interaction.

In the context of courage, integrity ensures that our actions align with our inner convictions. It allows us to make difficult choices, even when the consequences are unfavorable, because we know that staying true to our values is more important than immediate comfort or approval. Integrity strengthens courage by providing a moral compass, helping us navigate the complexities of life with consistency and authenticity.

Compassion, on the other hand, is the ability to empathize with others' suffering and respond with kindness, understanding, and support. Compassion does not simply mean feeling sorry for others—it means actively seeking to alleviate their pain, to offer comfort, and to stand by them in times of need. Compassion is a form of courage because it requires vulnerability.

It asks us to open our hearts to others, to risk emotional exposure, and to offer help even when we may not know how or when our efforts will be reciprocated.

When combined, integrity and compassion create a balanced form of courage. Integrity ensures that we act with honesty and fairness, while compassion helps us remain connected to the humanity of others. Together, these elements allow us to lead with both strength and empathy, facing the world's challenges with a sense of moral clarity and a commitment to the well-being of others.

5.7.3: Leadership and Strength in Adversity

Leadership is often associated with the ability to inspire, direct, and guide others toward a shared goal. True leadership, however, is not about control or authority; it is about service, responsibility, and the courage to act on behalf of others, especially in times of crisis or difficulty. Leaders demonstrate courage by taking initiative, making tough decisions, and bearing the weight of responsibility for their team or community. Leadership requires a combination of vision, empathy, and strength—a willingness to be vulnerable, to listen, and to support others, while also having the resolve to make difficult decisions when necessary.

Strength in adversity is the ability to maintain resolve, stay focused, and persevere even in the most challenging circumstances. It is easy to be courageous when the path is clear and the outcome is favorable. However, true strength reveals itself when we are faced with hardship, loss, or uncertainty. It is the ability to remain calm in a storm, to make decisions under pressure, and to continue moving forward even when the odds seem insurmountable.

In the face of adversity, courage is not always about dramatic actions; sometimes it is about the quiet, steadfast determination to keep going. Strength in adversity requires emotional resilience—the ability to manage stress, to recover from setbacks, and to maintain hope even when the situation seems bleak. It is the courage to keep moving, one step at a time, knowing that each small action contributes to overcoming the larger challenge.

When combined, leadership and strength in adversity create a powerful form of courage that can inspire and uplift others. A leader who demonstrates strength in adversity not only shows their own courage but also instills confidence and hope in those they lead. Their actions remind others that, even in the face of hardship, it is possible to rise above and continue striving toward a better future.

5.7.4: Embracing the Unknown and Taking Action

One of the most fundamental aspects of courage is the willingness to embrace the unknown. The unknown represents all that is uncertain, unpredictable, and potentially dangerous in life. It is the vast, uncharted territory that lies beyond our comfort zones. It is also the place where growth, innovation, and transformation occur. To embrace the unknown is to accept that life is full of uncertainty and that we must be willing to step into that uncertainty with faith and courage.

Embracing the unknown requires a mindset shift. It involves letting go of the need for control and certainty, and instead trusting that we have the capacity to navigate whatever challenges arise. It means stepping into new experiences, exploring new ideas, and being open to new possibilities, even when the outcome is unclear. Embracing the unknown is the first step in any act of courage—it is the willingness to face fear and take risks, knowing that there is no guarantee of success.

Taking action is the natural complement to embracing the unknown. Courage is not simply about thinking or feeling; it is about doing. Taking action is the manifestation of courage in the world. It is the willingness to move forward, to make decisions, and to act on our beliefs, even when we are unsure of the outcome. Action is what transforms potential into reality—it is the bridge between intention and accomplishment.

When we embrace the unknown and take action, we open ourselves to new opportunities, growth, and learning. Even if the outcome is not what we expected, the act of moving forward teaches us valuable lessons. Action, fueled by courage, allows us to take control of our destiny, to shape our lives, and to make an impact in the world.

Embracing the Full Spectrum of Courage

Courage is not a singular, static force; it is a dynamic, evolving quality that encompasses many elements. Self-confidence and conviction, integrity and compassion, leadership and strength in adversity, and embracing the unknown and taking action are the building blocks that form the foundation of true courage. Each element contributes to our ability to face fear, uncertainty, and challenge with grace and resilience.

As we cultivate these elements in our lives, we develop a more comprehensive understanding of courage—not as a reaction to external threats, but as an ongoing practice that shapes our character, our relationships, and our ability to navigate the complexities of life. Courage is not just about overcoming fear; it is about living authentically, making difficult choices, and standing firm in our beliefs, no matter the obstacles in our path. By embracing these elements of courage, we empower ourselves to live with purpose, integrity, and a deep commitment to the values that matter most.

Epilogue: The Ever-Expanding Horizon of Being

As we close the pages of this exploration, we are reminded that philosophy is not merely an intellectual pursuit but an experience, a lived journey through the vast expanse of thought, feeling, and presence. We began by asking questions, questioning what we thought we knew, and ultimately discovering that the answers are not out there, waiting to be found, but within, quietly unfolding as we evolve.

The very essence of being is elusive, intangible, yet it is the most profound truth we carry with us. This journey has sought to illuminate the space between thought and reality, between mind and matter, between you and the universe. It is not an end but a continuation, a shift in perception that urges us to go beyond the surface of our experiences and into the depths of our own consciousness.

The framework of being, as we have explored, is both a construct and a reality. It is the dance of thought and feeling, an intricate rhythm that shapes our every moment. As we move through the world, we are constantly creating, recreating, and dissolving our reality through the very thoughts we hold. In the dance of thought and feeling, we find the pulse of life itself—the force that propels us forward, whether we are aware of it or not.

But awareness, as we have come to understand, is key. It is the gateway to presence, to truly living and experiencing life in its fullest capacity. The philosophy of presence calls us to stop, to breathe, and to recognize that this moment is all there is. In this space, the past and future fade away, and we are left with the purity of now. This presence, however fleeting, is the truest form of connection to the universe and to ourselves.

And connection—this is perhaps the most profound realization we can take from this journey. It is the thread that weaves all things together. From the connections between our thoughts and our feelings, to the bonds we share with others, to our relationship with the divine, connection is the foundation of all experience. The role of connection, whether to others or to the universe at large, shapes the very fabric of our being. It is through connection that we find meaning, that we find purpose, and that we find our way home to ourselves.

In the journey ahead, we are called to recognize that we are not separate from the world around us. We are not isolated entities but part of a greater whole, an ever-expanding universe of consciousness. To step forward on this path is to embrace the interconnectedness of all things, to honor the sacredness of each moment, and to walk in the knowledge that every step we take is part of a much larger dance.

We are called to presence. To stop and listen. To hear the whispers of the universe, the quiet voice within that tells us we are enough, that we are worthy, and that we are the creators of our own reality. This is not a call to passivity but to active participation in the creation of our lives. It is a call to awaken from the slumber of conditioned thought and to rise into the full brilliance of our own consciousness.

The concept of "God is You" is not one of blind devotion or external worship but a radical recognition that the divine resides within each of us. We are the origin of our own experiences, the creators of our own destiny. Thought is not just something we do; it is something we are. And in this realization, we discover that the power we seek is already within us, waiting to be harnessed. The illusion of faith is shattered when we understand that faith is not something outside of us but the very essence of our being, the energy that flows through us, that drives us forward, that connects us to the infinite.

The healing power of thought, the power of asking, and the devotion to passion are all facets of this realization. We are not mere passengers on the journey of life but active participants, co-creators of the world we inhabit. As we expand our horizon and step into the fullness of who we are, we realize that the cycle of God, of creation, is ever-present. We are constantly in the process of becoming, of evolving, of shaping our own reality.

In the exploration of language, we have seen that it is not just a tool for communication but a powerful force for creation. Language shapes our reality, molds our perceptions, and gives voice to our deepest thoughts and desires. Words are not merely symbols; they are expressions of energy, of thought, of intention. Through language, we connect, we innovate, and we bridge the gap between the seen and the unseen, the known and the unknown.

The ethical use of language is a reminder that with great power comes great responsibility. The words we speak, the stories we tell, the expressions we use all have the potential to shape the world around us. Language is not neutral; it is a force that can uplift or destroy, heal or harm. It is through language that we express our deepest truths, our greatest fears, and our highest aspirations.

As we turn to the deeper layers of our existence—the body, the mind, the physiological needs, and the reality of fear—we come to understand that all of these are interconnected. Our thoughts, our feelings, our physical bodies, and our minds are not separate entities but part of a greater whole. Fear, as we have explored, is not something to be avoided but something to be understood. It is a guide, a teacher, a messenger that points us toward what we need to face in order to grow. And acceptance, as we have learned, is the key to unlocking the door to freedom. It is through acceptance that we find peace, that we find clarity, and that we find the strength to move forward.

Respect, passion, and courage are the pillars upon which we build our lives.

Respect for ourselves, for others, and for the world around us is the foundation of all meaningful connection. Passion is the fire that drives us, the energy that propels us forward, and the fuel that keeps us moving toward our highest potential. Courage is the willingness to face the unknown, to step into the uncertainty, and to trust that we are supported by the universe in all that we do.

Mukti, the idea of liberation, is not an abstract concept but a living reality. It is the freedom that comes when we let go of the stories that bind us, when we release the limitations we have placed on ourselves, and when we embrace the fullness of who we are. Mukti is the ultimate freedom—the freedom to be, to exist, to create, and to love without fear or hesitation.

In the end, the journey of philosophy is not about finding answers but about asking the right questions. It is about recognizing that we are all part of a grand and eternal dance, and that every step we take, every thought we think, and every word we speak is part of the creation of our reality. The art of being is not a destination but a journey, one that unfolds with each breath, each moment, and each realization. And as we continue on this journey, may we always remember that the horizon is ever-expanding, and the possibilities are limitless.

Becoming the Divine You

Exploring the Depths of Human Thought and Inquiry

What is the meaning of existence? How have the greatest minds shaped our understanding of truth, ethics, and reality? This book delves into the rich history and profound ideas of philosophy, tracing the evolution of human thought from ancient wisdom to modern intellectual debates.

Through the lens of the **Becoming The Divine You,** this book explores the impact of philosophy on society, education, politics, and science. It highlights the contributions of legendary thinkers, the significance of philosophical movements, and the role of critical inquiry in shaping our world.

Whether you are a seasoned philosopher, a student of knowledge, or simply curious about life's biggest questions, this book offers insights, discussions, and reflections that will challenge your perspective and inspire deeper contemplation.

Discover:

- The origins and evolution of philosophical thought
- The key figures and schools of philosophy
- The role of Divinity in shaping societies
- Thought-provoking debates and ethical dilemmas

Join the journey of wisdom and reflection—because philosophy is not just about questions, but about the way we live our lives.